# A
# STRAY CAT
# IS IN
# DISTRESS!

The warm breeze ruffles my hair. I can hear the sounds of my parents' guests downstairs. Someone is singing another song, this time in English, and everyone joins in on the chorus. But suddenly I am distracted by a sound from below: it is a thin, urgent wailing. No, not wailing. Meowing! It must be the ginger cat. I know it in my bones. Did she have her kittens? Is she in trouble and crying for help? I look down at the box in the yard. It is empty, but still the meowing continues. Where can she be? I grab Bernadette Louise, and hurry back downstairs to find out.

## OTHER BOOKS YOU MAY ENJOY

# The Cats
## in the
# DOLL SHOP

*by*

YONA ZELDIS McDONOUGH

*illustrated by*

HEATHER MAIONE

PUFFIN BOOKS
An Imprint of Penguin Group (USA) Inc.

*In memory of my grandmother Tania Brightman:*

*tiny, fierce, and fiercely missed*—Y. Z. M.

ଔ

*To my sister Carla*—H. M.

PUFFIN BOOKS
Published by the Penguin Group
Penguin Young Readers Group, 345 Hudson Street, New York, New York 10014, U.S.A.
Penguin Group (Canada), 90 Eglinton Avenue East, Suite 700, Toronto, Ontario, Canada M4P 2Y3
(a division of Pearson Penguin Canada Inc.)
Penguin Books Ltd, 80 Strand, London WC2R 0RL, England
Penguin Ireland, 25 St Stephen's Green, Dublin 2, Ireland (a division of Penguin Books Ltd)
Penguin Group (Australia), 250 Camberwell Road, Camberwell, Victoria 3124, Australia
(a division of Pearson Australia Group Pty Ltd)
Penguin Books India Pvt Ltd, 11 Community Centre, Panchsheel Park, New Delhi – 110 017, India
Penguin Group (NZ), 67 Apollo Drive, Rosedale, Auckland 0632, New Zealand
(a division of Pearson New Zealand Ltd.)
Penguin Books (South Africa) (Pty) Ltd, 24 Sturdee Avenue, Rosebank, Johannesburg 2196, South Africa

Penguin Books Ltd, Registered Offices: 80 Strand, London WC2R 0RL, England

First published in the United States of America by Viking,
a division of Penguin Young Readers Group, 2011
Published by Puffin Books, a member of Penguin Young Readers Group, 2012

1 3 5 7 9 10 8 6 4 2

Text copyright © Yona Zeldis McDonough, 2011
Illustrations copyright © Heather Maione, 2011

THE LIBRARY OF CONGRESS HAS CATALOGED THE VIKING EDITION AS FOLLOWS:
McDonough, Yona Zeldis.
The cats in the doll shop / by Yona Zeldis McDonough ; illustrated by Heather Maione.
p. cm.
Summary: With World War I raging in Europe, eleven-year-old Anna is thrilled to learn that her cousin
Tania is coming from Russia to stay with Anna's family on the lower East Side of New York, and although
Tania is shy and withdrawn when she arrives, her love of cats helps her adjust to her new family.
ISBN 978-0-670-01279-4 (hc)
[1. Immigrants—New York (State)—New York—Fiction. 2. Cats—Fiction. 3. Cousins—Fiction.
4. Dolls—Fiction. 5. Jews—United States—Fiction.
6. New York (N.Y.)—History—1898-1951—Fiction.]
I. Maione, Heather Harms, ill. II. Title.
PZ7.M15655Cat 2011      [Fic]—dc22      2011009312

Puffin Books ISBN 978-0-14-242198-7

Printed in the United States of America

Book design by Nancy Brennan      Set in Kennerly

# CONTENTS

# I

## WORDS FROM FAR AWAY

It all starts with the letters. Not that letters, all by themselves, are such an odd thing. Papa and Mama run Breittlemann's Doll Shop, where they make dolls, and they get letters all the time: from Mr. Greenfield, the buyer at the big, fancy toy store uptown called F.A.O. Schwarz, and from buyers at other stores, too. There are letters from suppliers of the different materials they use: velvet and cotton, wool and felt. Sometimes they get letters from people who have bought one of the dolls and want to know if there are any new models available.

But the letters I am talking about are different. They come all the way from Russia, where Mama and Papa were born, and they arrive in fragile envelopes that tear when they are opened. My sisters and I can't read what is in the letters, because they are written in Yiddish, which is the language both of my parents' families spoke back in what Mama calls the "old country." Sophie, my big sister, can understand Yiddish when she hears it spoken, but even she—a regular smarty-pants, all A's and gold stars at school—cannot understand the words, which are written in Hebrew letters and crowded onto the thin, pearl gray sheets of paper.

First the letters come only once in a while. Then we begin to notice that they are coming every week, sometimes even twice a week. Mama rips the envelopes in her haste to open them—did I mention they are fragile?—and all the features on her face seem to draw together, as if pulled tight by a thread, as she reads. Sometimes she looks worried long after she has finished reading the letters. Tonight is one of those times.

"What's wrong, Mama?" asks Trudie, my younger sister. It is a Sunday in August, and we're all sitting together at our small, crowded table. Dinner—cold beet soup called borscht, with dumplings and bread—is over, and I am wondering if Mama will let us go downstairs and play in the doll shop. Even though we girls are getting older—Trudie is nine, I'm eleven, and Sophie is thirteen—we still like to play with our dolls.

"Nothing's wrong," Mama says to Trudie. But the tone of her voice lets me know this is not true, and because of this, I don't ask to go downstairs after all. I decide to stay up here, so I can keep an eye on what is happening. And sure enough, after Sophie and I have finished doing the dinner dishes, Mama calls us all together in the tiny parlor that is just off the kitchen. Papa sits in his chair on one side of the room. Mama sits in her chair on the other. But instead of the sewing basket she usually brings out in the evenings, she has the letters—all of them it seems—fanned out in her lap.

"Girls, we are going to have a visitor," Mama says.

"A visitor? Who is it?" Trudie asks.

"Is it someone we know?" asks Sophie.

"Not yet," Mama says, glancing over at Papa. "But you'll get to know her soon. In fact, you'll get to know her very well."

"Tell us who it is, Mama!" Trudie pleads.

"It's your cousin Tania," Mama says.

"She's Aunt Rivka's daughter," I say. Mama has told us about her. "She and I have exactly the same birthday and we're exactly the same age. You said it was a coincidence that you and your sister both had baby girls on the very same day."

"That's right, Anna!" says Mama.

"So what's she like?" Sophie asks me, as if she didn't quite believe it when I said I remembered hearing about her.

"Well, she has blonde hair . . ." I begin. I am not actually sure about this, but when I speak again, I try to make my voice sound very confident anyway. "Long blonde hair and bright blue eyes. Blue as . . ." I have to think for a minute. "Blue as forget-me-nots."

"You've never even *seen* a forget-me-not," says Sophie. She tosses her own shining brown hair—always brushed, always neat, and always perfect—back over her shoulders.

"How do you know?" I say hotly. Sophie and I get along pretty well most of the time, but every now and then she acts like she knows everything and I know just about nothing. I don't know why it's important to me to insist that Tania is blonde and blue-eyed. Maybe it's because I know Sophie wishes she were both.

"That's enough, girls," says Mama. "Tania does have blonde hair, or at least she did when she was a baby. It might have gotten darker by now. And Rivka says her eyes are very blue. But that's not what's important right now."

"What *is* important, Mama?" Trudie asks. She is clutching her doll, Angelica Grace, to her chest. "The reason she's coming here?"

"Yes, that's it," says Mama. "The reason that she's coming here." Mama puts her arm around Trudie. "You see, her papa died when she was a baby, and she has no brothers and sisters. So for a long time, it was just Rivka and Tania, living together in their little village. But now Aunt Rivka wants to move to the city. She's going to be a maid in a very fine house in Moscow."

"Isn't that a good thing?" I ask. I know about the Great War that is still going on in Europe. Papa has said that jobs are scarce, and so I would think Aunt Rivka is lucky to have found one.

"It is, except the house where Rivka will be working has no place for Tania."

"Then where will she live if she can't live with her mother?" asks Trudie. She runs a finger across her doll's smooth, painted face.

"That's exactly why she's going to come to live here," says Papa, leaning forward in his chair. "And if she lives here, she'll be able to go to school, like you girls do. She'll learn to read and write and add and subtract. That means she'll have some choices about what she wants to do when she's grown up—just like all of you."

"I'm going to be a teacher," Sophia declares.

"And I'm going to be a ballerina!" adds Trudie. Trudie does love to dance.

"You can't just decide to *be* a ballerina," Sophie says. "You have to study for a long, long time."

"Oh well," says Trudie. "So I won't be a ballerina. I'll be an actress then. Or a singer." She seems to consider the possibilities. "I know—a nurse! Just like Nurse Nora." With her jaunty little outfit and sweet, caring expression, Nurse Nora is the most popular of the dolls we make in the shop.

I can see that Sophie does not believe any of this. She has that I'm-so-grown-up look on her face. Maybe

I shouldn't even say what I want to be. Sophie will find some way to make me think it's not possible. Or that it's silly. But I decide I don't care.

"I'm going to be a writer," I announce boldly. "I'll write stories and poems and maybe even plays." Everyone turns to look at me. "My books will be published in beautiful leather-covered volumes with gold lettering on the front. People everywhere will read them. They'll be in libraries all over the city. No, all over the country."

I happen to love libraries. Once a week, I walk up to the Tompkins Square Library on Tenth Street where I can check out books. I have my very own library card. The librarian, Miss Abbott, is so nice. She sets aside things she thinks I will like. She's always right, too. What if one day Miss Abbott were able to give a book I wrote to some other little girl coming through those doors? Wouldn't I feel proud!

"Those are all fine dreams," says Mama. "If you work hard in school, you'll make them come true. And Tania— we want her to have a chance to dream, too."

"How long will she be staying?" Sophie wants to know. "Will we have enough room for her?" I have to admit these are good questions. Our apartment has only four small rooms—kitchen, parlor, and two bedrooms.

"Your mother and I have talked about that," Papa says, glancing over at Mama. From that glance, I can tell that some of the conversations haven't been so smooth. "Tania will be here with us for about a year," he continues.

"A year! That's a long time," says Sophie.

"Aunt Rivka needs that much time to make the money for her own passage," Mama says. "And then she'll come over, too, and we'll help her find an apart-ment of her own nearby."

"It's going to be crowded," Trudie says. Sophie nods vigorously.

"Yes," Mama says, lifting her chin a little. "It will be. And it may not be easy to have another girl living in your room."

"We'll manage," I tell Mama. "You can count on us." Sophie and Trudie don't say a thing. "When will she be here?"

"That's what Rivka and I are trying to arrange now," says Mama. "I'll let you know as soon we've figured it out."

Shortly after that conversation, September starts and with it, school. Trudie is in fourth grade now. She has the same teacher I had back when I was in that class. Sophie is in eighth grade, her last year in our school. Next year she'll be in high school, which seems impossibly grown up to me. And I'm in sixth grade, right smack in the middle, where I always am.

I begin to take more careful notice of the letters. I ask Mama what they say, so she reads them to us at night, after our lessons are done. It seems I have more schoolwork than last year. History, arithmetic, geography, spelling, and reading—my favorite. Sometimes I don't finish until late, and so Mama reads the letters while we are already in bed. Of course she has to translate from the Yiddish, or Trudie and I won't understand.

"July 7, 1915," reads Mama one night just after school has started. She smooths the thin sheet of paper with her hand. "Today I went into town to get the papers Tania will need to make the trip. I'll fill them out and then next week, I'll deliver them to the proper office."

"July?" says Trudie. "It's already September." She leans over to get closer to the letter—not that she can read it anyway—and her elbow pokes me in the side. *Ouch.* My sisters and I sleep together in one big bed. I didn't mind so much when we were little, but now that we are getting bigger, I wish we didn't have to share. Papa says since Tania is coming, he will be getting us new beds, one for each of us. No more sharing! I am looking forward to *that*.

"It takes time for the letters to get here," Mama explains. "A long time."

"Keep going," I say, inching away from Trudie as best I can. "What else does she say?" So Mama continues reading, and even though I can sense my sisters losing interest, I want to hear every word. I crane my neck so I can see the foreign letters on the page.

"Mama," I ask. "Will Tania be able to speak English?"

"No," Mama answers. "So I hope that's something you girls can help her with—learning English."

"I can do that," Sophie says, rather boastfully in my

opinion. "I'm going to be a teacher, remember?"

"That would be wonderful," Mama says. "Just what we need."

I don't say anything, but privately I think that if Sophie is going to act like a know-it-all with our cousin, she isn't going to be much help to her.

To my surprise, the next day there is another letter. Mama reads it to us after supper. "Tania's application was finally approved. Now I have to buy the ticket and start packing." As I listen, I wonder if Tania has a favorite doll. Will she bring it along with her? Then I wonder if she has a doll at all. For a long time, Sophie, Trudie, and I did not have dolls of our own, even though our parents had a doll repair shop. Dolls, especially bisque and porcelain dolls, are very costly. We used to play with the dolls our father fixed, but we did not own them.

Then the Great War broke out in Europe. America sided against Germany. All of the doll parts Papa used for repairs came from Germany. Because of the war, the parts were no longer available. Some of the dolls, including the ones we named Bernadette Louise, Victoria Marie, and Angelica Grace, were abandoned by their owners. It was only for that reason that we were able to keep them. Now Mama and Papa do not fix dolls but make them instead. They produce Nurse Nora—who was *my* idea and is now everyone's favorite—and also a fairy doll and a queen doll.

Mama told us that Aunt Rivka is poor, and it has taken her a long time to save the money for Tania's ticket. So I am pretty sure that Tania will not have a doll, or even if she does, it will not be a very nice one. Well, if Sophie decided that she will be Tania's English teacher, I decide that I will be the one to help her get a doll. Maybe it will be one of the dolls that Papa and Mama make. If I ask Papa, he will probably let Tania have Nurse Nora. I wonder if Tania would like her.

But then I get another idea. A much better idea. I will *make* a doll for Tania, all by myself. A Russian princess? A Spanish dancer? A bride with a long train and a lace veil? I don't know yet. But what I do know is that she will be a very special doll, a gift to my cousin that comes straight from my heart.

# 2

## OUT BACK

Although the big calendar Papa keeps posted in the doll shop says September 1915, the days are as beautiful, warm, and golden as summer. I lag behind my sisters on the way to school, wishing I could stay outside and play instead of going inside to join my class. And on the way home, I let them get even farther ahead, stopping to look in all the shop windows along the way. There's a shop that sells only buttons, and another that sells hats of all kinds. My favorite is the store that sells the prettiest undergarments for ladies and girls. I love the frilly petticoats and delicate camisoles, the embroidered nightdresses and matching robes. I wish I could buy Mama a set like that for her birthday.

When I get to the candy store at the corner of Hester Street, I check my pocket. Empty—too bad. If I had any money from my allowance—two cents a week—I would stop for a soda or a milk shake.

When I finally do get home, I still don't want to go inside, so I head out in back of the shop, where there is the barest sliver of a yard with hard, parched dirt that grows exactly nothing. Even the weeds struggle back here.

"There you are!" I turn to see Sophie, who has followed me outside. "Trudie and I have been home for an hour. We were wondering where you were."

"I came home a different way," I tell her.

"I've just about finished my lessons. You haven't even started yours yet," Sophie says.

"In a minute," I tell her.

"Suit yourself," says Sophie, and goes back inside.

I sigh. There was a time not so long ago when I thought Sophie was beginning to view me not as a little sister but as an equal. Lately though, it seems she has gone back to thinking that I am just so far behind.

Sophie is changing, both outside and in. She has gotten taller, and though it pains me to admit it, even prettier. She no longer wears her hair in braids and is occasionally allowed to wear it up, like when we go to *shul* on the holidays or when Mama and Papa invite company for dinner. And on her last birthday, Mama gave her a pair of earrings with real garnets at the center. The dark red stones glow against Sophie's pale skin. I am so jealous of those earrings! They belonged to Mama's own mother, and Mama says when I am a little older, she will give me a pair, too, but it is hard to wait.

Is it any wonder that I sometimes need to be by my-self, even if that means sitting in the drab, cramped yard, looking up at the backs of the neighboring buildings and the network of black metal fire escapes that are attached to them? There is another tiny yard directly behind ours, separated by a brick wall. At the end of that yard is a building much like the one we live in. The view is pretty dull, but I continue to look at it anyway, because there is nothing else to look at.

So that is how I happened to see her—the big ginger-colored kitty padding along the third-story fire escape at-tached to the building just behind ours. Judging from her swollen belly, I am almost sure that she is going to have kittens. Soon. In fact, I'll bet she is probably looking for a place to have them right now.

Immediately, I head back into the shop, where the three worktables are covered with scraps of fabric and dolls in different stages of production. Papa is cutting the twine on a box. Mama is attaching capes to Nurse Nora dolls. Our two new employees, Kathleen and Michael O'Leary, are busy working on other dolls. Michael gives me a little wave. I smile back, but I don't stop to chat.

"Sophie!" I call. "Sophie! Trudie! Come quick."

Trudie comes right away, but Sophie doesn't answer. So I lead Trudie out back, where the cat is now sitting on the fire escape.

"Look!" I say, pointing upward.

"What?" Trudie does not see.

"There! I wave my arm excitedly. "That big orange cat. Don't you see her?"

"I do now!" says Trudie. "But why is she so fat?"

"She's going to have kittens," I explain. "And she's looking for a good place to have them."

"The fire escape doesn't seem like a very good place," Trudie says.

"The fire escape doesn't seem like a very good place for what?" Sophie comes out into the yard. She has arranged her hair in a new way, with two small braids wound around her head and secured with pins. The rest, long and loose, hangs down her back. Where did she get the idea for *that*? The style makes her look a bit unfamiliar. And older, too.

"Doesn't seem like a good place to have kittens," says Trudie.

"Who's having kittens?"

Together, Trudie and I point to the ginger cat, who is now pacing nervously across the fire escape.

"Trudie, go get that box that's under the table by the window," Sophie says. Then she turns to me. "Can you find something soft and warm, Anna? One of the rags Mama uses for cleaning. Or even two?"

Trust Sophie to waltz in late and start taking over like she is the one in charge. Still, I can see what she has in mind—a bed for the soon-to-be-mother cat. And she did ask me very nicely about the rags. So I run upstairs in search of the rag basket.

Inside, Mama is in the kitchen making supper. One of our neighbors, Mrs. Kornblatt, is sitting at the table. She and Mama are chattering away and take no notice of me. I slip past them and dig through the rag basket, where I find two pieces of faded blue flannel. Perfect to line a cat bed. I go downstairs to where Trudie is waiting with the box, but I don't see Sophie. I lay the flannel inside.

"Do you think the cat will come down here?" Trudie asks.

"We need something to lure her," I say.

"I've got just the thing," says Sophie, walking back into the yard with a bag on her arm. "Look." She pulls out a tiny pitcher filled with cream, and a saucer.

"Where did you get that?" Trudie asks. Cream is a luxury in our home. Mama does not buy it often.

"I took just a little while Mama was busy talking to Mrs. Kornblatt."

"What if she finds out?" Trudie asks.

"It's for a good cause," Sophie says. "She'll understand."

I ponder that. Papa and Mama are in favor of good causes, and encourage us to perform small acts of *tzedakah*—charity—whenever we can.

"Well, I guess it will be all right then. . . ." Trudie says.

"Of course it will," says Sophie. "Just look at her! Don't you think she needs help?"

The cat sits down on her haunches. She seems to be looking directly at me with her big, amber eyes. I look back at her. Yes, I decide. Sophie is right.

We set the box near the brick wall and place the saucer of cream next to it.

"How will she get over the wall to reach the box?" asks Trudie.

"Cats are good climbers," I say.

"Even cats that are going to have kittens?"

Trudie has a point. But we can't get over the wall, so we have no other choice.

"If she really wants to, she can climb over," Sophie says.

Just at that moment, we hear our mother's voice. "Trudie! Anna! Sophie!" she called. "Time for supper! Come inside to wash your hands."

"My hands are *clean*," grumbles Trudie, but she follows us to the sink just the same.

When we are all seated round the small oak table in our little kitchen, Mama sets the blue-and-white platter of corned beef and cabbage down in front of us. Fragrant steam rises off the food.

While I am mopping up the tasty liquid from the cabbage with a slice of fresh rye bread, Mama tells us about the most recent letter she received from Aunt Rivka. Tania's boat is sailing on the fifteenth of September. Today is the fourth—that's eleven days off.

"That means she'll be here soon!" I exclaim. "But not for Rosh Hashanah." Rosh Hashanah, the Jewish new year, is on the eighth, and Mama has invited a few people over for dinner to celebrate with us: our next door neighbors the Kleins, Mrs. Schwebel, a widow from our *shul*, and Mr. Umansky, one of Papa's old friends.

"No, not for the holiday," says Mama. She begins to clear the plates and sets out the bowl of stewed fruit for dessert.

"How long does it take to get here on the boat?" Trudie asks.

"The crossing takes about two weeks," Mama replies.

"Which is not as long as when we did it," Papa points out. He helps himself and then passes the bowl around.

"So if she leaves on the fifteenth, that means she'll get here on the twenty-ninth," I say, doing the arithmetic in my head.

"The date is not exact," Mama says, taking a spoonful of her fruit. "It's just an approximation. We'll look for the notice of the ship's arrival in the newspaper. That's where it's announced."

When we have all finished dessert, I help Mama clean up while Sophie and Trudie work on their lessons. Our kitchen is compact but efficient. It contains a deep sink—the only one we have, so we use it for washing up, brushing our teeth, and filling our water pitcher. We are lucky to have both a stove and an icebox. Not all our neighbors do. And our bathtub is in the kitchen, covered with a hinged piece of wood when we are not using it. Mama stands a folding screen in front of it whenever someone takes a bath.

"Mama, tell me about the crossing," I say as I bring the plates to the sink. The word has stayed with me ever since Mama said it at supper; it makes the ocean journey sound like a grand adventure. I know my parents made "the crossing" years ago, before they had us or even had met each other. Papa came with his mother and two brothers. Mama's parents had died, so she came with her aunt, uncle, and cousins. But I don't know the details. "Was it exciting? Was it fun?"

"Fun?" Mama turns to look at me. "No, I wouldn't have called it fun. The boat was filthy and crowded. Sometimes the ocean was rough. There were big storms that made the waves swell. We were so frightened. And on top of that, everyone got seasick."

"Did you?" I ask.

"Almost every day," she says. "It was terrible. Throwing up, headaches—I was never so sick in my life." She stops washing the plate she is holding.

"That does sound terrible," I say.

"And here's something I haven't thought of in years." Mama puts the plate in the dish rack and sits down on a chair. "I had a doll with me on the trip. Just a little rag doll, but she was the only doll I had. My mother had made her for me when I was just a tiny girl."

"Really?" Mama never told me this before. "What was her name?"

"Suki." Mama smiles. "Isn't that a funny name? She had two little black buttons for eyes, and her mouth was a red X that had been sewn on with embroidery thread."

"You must have loved her," I say.

"I did," Mama agrees. "And when we were on the boat, I lost her."

"Lost her!" I exclaim. "How sad!"

"It was," says Mama. "I cried and cried. My aunt made me another doll, but it wasn't the same." She gets up from the chair. "Well, the dishes aren't going to get done by sitting around and thinking about the past, are they?" She reaches for another plate. "I only hope Tania has a better time of it. She won't have her mother or an aunt with her, after all. She'll be with a friend of Aunt Rivka's. . . ." sighs Mama.

As soon as we are through in the kitchen. I go in search of my books so I can start my spelling lesson.

"The crossing" no longer sounds like a great adventure. Instead, it sounds, well, awful. I am glad I do not have to do it. But Tania does. Before I settle down to work, I take Bernadette Louise from her place in our room. She always makes me feel better when I am worried about something. Looking at her smooth, glazed face, I realize that she made a "crossing," too, when she was first brought over from Germany. And although she is not human, the trip was still dangerous. She could easily have gotten broken or lost. Instead, she had a safe trip and ended up here with me. I find myself wishing, hard, that Tania will be as lucky.

# 3

## $\mathcal{A}$ SWEET YEAR

We have just finished our poetry lesson in school when the dismissal bell rings. I stuff my pencils, books, and papers into my satchel and hurry home with my sisters. We immediately head out through the shop, where Kathleen and Michael are working, to the yard, to check on the cat. She is nowhere to be seen. The box we prepared yesterday is empty, and the cream is untouched except for a few flecks of soot that have settled on its surface. Trudie and I are both horrified as we watch Sophie pour it into the dirt.

"Well, we can't give her cream that's been sitting out all night, can we? It may be spoiled."

I suppose she is right, though the waste of it bothers

me. But the absence of the cat bothers me even more.

"Where do you suppose she went?" I ask Sophie. "She looked like she was going to have those kittens soon."

"I know," Sophie says. "But we've done everything we can, haven't we?"

"Maybe we can try to tempt her with something else," I say. "Something she won't be able to resist."

"Mama said we're having fish soup tonight," Trudie pipes up. "I'll bet she's upstairs in the kitchen making it right now."

"Cats love fish," Sophie declares in that know-it-all way of hers. She turns to Trudie. "If Mama is making fish soup, there will be fish scraps. Go inside and get some from the garbage pail."

"I don't want to," whines Trudie.

"Why not?" Sophie demands.

"They smell so bad," Trudie says.

"So what?" Sophie admonishes. "The cat will think those smelly old scraps are the most delicious treat in the world." Trudie stops whining and goes inside.

While she is gone, I look over at the third-story fire escape where we saw the cat yesterday.

"What's that?" I ask Sophie.

"What's what?"

"That gray thing. In the corner."

She follows my gaze upward. "It looks like a blanket."

I nod. It *is* a blanket.

"Do you think someone left it there for the cat?" I ask. Sophie and I continue to look.

"No," she says finally. "It's not folded or laid out nicely. It's just stuffed in the corner. As if it's trash." And I have to agree.

Trudie returns with the fish scraps in a clean saucer.

"Did Mama ask you what you wanted them for?" Sophie asks.

"I took them from the garbage. Just like you said. She didn't notice."

"Good," says Sophie, setting the saucer in the box.

"You don't want Mama and Papa to know what we're doing?" Trudie asks.

"Not exactly," Sophie.

"Why not?" I ask.

"You know how Papa is about cats and dogs living inside," Sophie reminds me. It's true. Whenever we have asked about getting a kitten or a puppy Papa has always said no. He told us how back in Russia, no one kept animals like that in the house. He said there were cats where he lived, but they had to catch their own food and never came inside. So he probably won't like our feeding this cat. With a last glance at the blanket on the fire escape across the yard, we troop inside to start our lessons.

In the days before Tania gets here, Mama doesn't receive any more letters from Aunt Rivka. But we have plenty to keep us busy. Rosh Hashanah is coming, and we all pitch in to prepare for the big dinner that Mama makes on the eve of the holiday.

There is a lot to do: polishing, ironing, sweeping, and dusting. We add two leaves to the table, so that there will be enough room for everyone to sit down. Mama roasts two chickens and bakes three round loaves of her delicious golden challah. She also prepares *tzimmes* with carrots, prunes and chunks of pumpkin; sponge cake; and slices of apple dipped in honey. Tradition says that this will make the new year sweet.

I don't have much time to think about Tania, or about the cat out back either. But when I do think of Tania,

I feel a pleasant tingle of anticipation. Since we are the same age, she won't act like a baby, the way Trudie still does at times. Just the other day, she scribbled on a drawing I was doing for school. When I told Papa, she burst out crying, like it was all my fault. And Tania won't treat *me* like a baby, the way Sophie sometimes does. No, with Tania, everything will be just right.

<hr/>

Our *erev* Rosh Hashanah dinner is a success. Mr. Umansky, Papa's friend from *shul*, presents me with a bouquet of flowers when I open the door. I giggle as I reach into the cabinet for a vase. Once we are seated, everyone exclaims over how pretty the table looks. Since I was the one to set it, I feel especially pleased. Mr. Klein eats three helpings of *tzimmes*, and we all devour Mama's delicious challah. Only a few crumbs, which Mama will scatter to the sparrows that gather on the sidewalk in front of the shop, are left. After dinner, some of the guests start singing songs that they learned in the old country. Mama sings a ballad in Yiddish. I don't understand the words, but the melody is so pretty it makes me go quiet for a few minutes. At the end, everyone claps, and I feel so proud of her.

The beautiful weather has continued, and even though it is nighttime, I have the sudden urge to go up on the roof. I ask my sisters if they want to join me. But Sophie doesn't want to, and Trudie is too tired. So I take Bernadette Louise under my arm and head up to the roof myself. I probably should ask my parents, but they are so busy with our company I decide I won't bother. Besides, I won't stay up there for very long.

Since the time Bernadette Louise actually became mine forever and always, I have sewed her several new outfits, including a tweed cape, a calico skirt and blouse, and a dark green corduroy suit. I've been sewing since I was a little girl. Mama, who can sew just about anything, taught all of us early on, and though I am not as talented as she is, the clothes turned out all right. Tonight Bernadette Louise wears a dress made from blue polished cotton with a red ribbon at her waist. The fabric was left over from material that Mama used for a dress of mine.

I sit down on the tarpaper surface of the roof, pulling my knees to my chest, and balance Bernadette Louise on top of them. I'm still thinking about the doll I plan to make for Tania. If I want to finish it before she arrives, I'd better come up with something soon. I ask

Bernadette Louise *her* ideas about what would be a good doll to make. Not that I expect her to answer me. I don't believe my doll can talk. But when I'm alone, I do like to talk to her. It helps me sort through things. I always feel better afterward.

The warm breeze ruffles my hair. I can hear the sounds of my parents' guests downstairs. Someone is singing another song, this time in English, and everyone joins in on the chorus. But suddenly I am distracted by a sound from below: it is a thin, urgent wailing. No, not wailing. Meowing! It must be the ginger cat. I know it in my bones. Did she have her kittens? Is she in trouble and crying for help? I look down at the box in the yard. It is empty, but still the meowing continues. Where can she be? I grab Bernadette Louise, and hurry back downstairs to find out.

# 4

## THE MAN WITH THE MUSTACHE

Trudie has already fallen asleep, but I find Sophie in the kitchen, nibbling on a piece of sponge cake. The rest of the guests have moved to the parlor, and so for a moment, we are alone.

"Put that down and come with me!" I say. Something about the tone of my voice makes her stuff the rest of the cake into her mouth as she follows me outside. The meowing of the cat is louder now. I tug on Sophie's arm and point. We see a man with a broom sweeping vigorously. He has a big handlebar mustache and a big belly hanging over his belt. Why is he out here at night sweeping?

The answer quickly becomes clear. Ginger Cat (for

that is now her name in my mind) must have had her kittens. Only instead of using the nice safe box we prepared for her, she went and gave birth on the gray blanket we saw stuffed in a corner of the fire escape. I can just make her out in the dark. I can also see some small shapes next to her—kittens! Clearly this man doesn't want them there, because he is sweeping them right off the fire escape and into the yard below!

Sophie clutches my hand fiercely as Ginger Cat and her kittens tumble from the fire escape, two stories down. Together, we both gasp out loud, as if we were one person. The man shakes out the blanket, and clutching it under his arm, climbs back into his apartment. We can hear the window shut with a loud *thud*. The meowing continues.

"Oh no!" Sophie moans. "How could he?"

"Let's call Papa," I say. "He'll know what to do." I can see Sophie hesitate. But the sound of the meowing is so pitiful that she agrees. We run back up the stairs alongside the doll shop to our apartment, where Papa is now playing a harmonica. "Papa, we need to see you right now!" Sophie says, her voice low and urgent.

"I was in the middle of playing for our guests," Papa says with a smile. "Can't it wait?"

"No, it can't," she says. I see her eyes pool with tears, and Papa must see it, too, because his smile fades as he turns to everyone and says, "Please excuse me. I'll be right back." Sophie never, ever cries, so if she is crying now, I think Papa must know there is a serious reason.

"What is it, Sophie?" he asks gently when we are alone. She turns to me and says, "You tell," before pressing a fist to her trembling mouth.

"Something terrible has happened, Papa," I say, grabbing his warm, comforting hand. "You have to come now, so you can see."

"Tell me what this terrible thing is," Papa says, but instead of answering, I lead him down the stairs and out the back door. We stand in the yard, where the sounds of meowing continue to pierce the velvety blue night.

"Cats meowing? Cats meow to communicate with each other. That's not so terrible," he says.

"Oh yes it is," I say, and I explain about the man, the broom, and the terrible fall from above.

All at once Papa stiffens. "Did the man have a thick mustache?" he asks. We nod, and Papa adds, "I know him. He runs a shoe repair shop on Hester Street. He's bad tempered and mean to his employees. And I've heard that he deliberately does shoddy work so people have to come back and pay for another repair. I'm not surprised to hear what he's done." The meowing continues. "Not surprised, but disgusted all the same. You girls were right to tell me."

Papa strides across the barren yard and pulls himself up and over the brick wall that separates it from the yard adjoining ours. Sophie and I sit down on the ground and wait. After about fifteen minutes, we hear Papa rustling in the yard behind ours, and once more, he is up and over the wall. This time, he stumbles as he lands. Then he picks himself up and brushes off his pants.

"Did you find them?" Sophie asks in a small voice. "Are they all right?" Her fist is back at her mouth again.

"I found the mother cat," says Papa. "She's fine."

"And what about the kittens?" I am not sure I want to hear the answer.

"I only found one kitten," Papa says carefully.

"But there were others. I saw them."

"They didn't survive the fall." Papa's face is grim as he delivers this news.

Sophie and I just look at each other, stricken.

"What about the one kitten you did find, Papa?" I say finally.

"He's alive. But I think he broke his back leg in the fall. It was dangling in a very peculiar way. It didn't look right to me," Papa says.

"That's so sad!" I burst out.

"Yes, it is," Papa agrees. "But his mother found him, and so at least he'll be fed."

"What about his leg?" I ask. "Do you think it will heal?"

"I don't know," Papa says.

"What if it doesn't?" Sophie asks.

"Well, the leg might wither and fall off," says Papa. "I saw that happen once, to a cat back in the old country. She hurt her leg in a fall from a roof. The leg just sort of hung there for a while. Eventually, it dropped off."

"That sounds terrible," Sophie says.

"Not as terrible as an infection. A cat can live with three legs. But an infection could kill him."

Sophie and I are silent, thinking about that for a moment.

"What will happen to the cats?" asks Sophie.

"There's not too much more we can do right now," Papa says. "We can leave scraps out for the mother. If she's hungry, she'll come and find them. Her kitten isn't ready to eat solid food yet anyway."

"We already set out some food," Sophie says. She shows Papa the box with the rags and the dish of fish scraps. Neither one of us mentions the cream.

"You girls can keep setting out scraps. But don't try to find the cats, and whatever you do, don't touch them. I don't want either one of you getting scratched. Or even worse—bitten." He turns to go inside.

Once Papa has gone, my sister turns to me and in a small, almost desperate voice says, "That man who swept the cats off the fire escape . . ."

"What about him?"

"How could he have been so cruel? How could anyone?"

"I don't know," I tell her. For a moment, it seems I am the big sister, and she is the younger one. I put my arms around her in a fierce hug, and just as fiercely, she hugs me back.

# 5

## Waiting

The next day, we get dressed up and go with our parents to the *shul* on Rivington Street. Sophie wears a velvet dress Mama made out of an old drape, and the garnet earrings. I wish I had a dress like that. Trudie and I wear nice dresses, too, made of black and ivory striped ticking. But they are not as nice as Sophie's dress. When I complain to Mama, she says that since Sophie is older and almost a young lady, it's important for her to start wearing more grown-up looking clothes. My turn will come, she tells me. I sigh. It feels like a long way off.

After *shul*, we don't go to school but back home where we spend time in the yard, looking for the cats. My friend Esther comes over, and we tell her everything that's happened—seeing Ginger Cat, the box, the food, the man with the mustache, the wounded kitten. Esther can't believe that the man could have been so cruel. "I think he should be arrested!" she says.

Ten days after Rosh Hashanah is Yom Kippur, the day of atonement. This year, Sophie decides that she will fast for the whole day, just like Mama and Papa. In the past, I felt grateful that we didn't have to do that. We girls would skip breakfast, go to *shul* in the morning, and then come home for lunch. I still don't want to fast all day, but I am not sure I like it that Sophie is moving away from us.

During the next couple of weeks, we keep a lookout for Ginger Cat and her kitten, but we don't see either of them. I even go up to the roof, because I think might be able to see better from up there.

The first time, I see nothing. I try again the next day, after school, and I am rewarded by the sight of the kitten nestled close to Ginger Cat. They are both lying near a stunted, nearly bare bush. The kitten doesn't have much fur, and he is as scrawny as the bush. Still, I wish I could pick him up and cuddle him. Ginger Cat looks very gentle and sweet lying there with her baby. Although Papa warned us, it's hard to believe she would ever scratch or bite.

I go for several more days without seeing him again. But the next time I spot the kitten from the roof, I notice something truly amazing. He is trying to stand up! He balances, shakily, on his three good legs. The fourth, with its useless paw, dangles behind him. I watch as he pulls himself up, then flops back down. He tries again, with the same result. Then he tries a third time, and manages to remain standing for several seconds longer. I am so proud of him! Although it is clearly hard, he is trying to stand up all by himself. And somehow I have not only the hope but the faith that he will be able to do it.

I also notice that he's starting to grow fur—he's like his mother in color, only lighter, as if someone has mixed white paint with the orange. I rush downstairs so I can tell my sisters. "Guess what I saw!" I say to Sophie and Trudie, who are in the kitchen peeling potatoes. I tell them all about the brave little cat who is just so, so, plucky—that's what he is! And then I realize: his name should be Plucky.

"Plucky," repeats Trudie, as if trying it on for size.

"I like it," says Sophie. "It fits." The glow of her approval stays with me for the rest of afternoon.

I have been so busy cat-watching that I almost forget that today is the twenty-eighth of September—that's the day when we are supposed to start checking the Shipping and Mails section of the newspaper. When we look, we see that Tania's boat is due to arrive tomorrow!

"Can we go with you to get her?" I ask Papa. He has finished working at his desk in the doll shop and is putting all his papers together. "Please?"

"You have to go to school," Papa says. "You'll see her when you get home."

That night, Sophie, Trudie, and I stay up talking long after lights out. This is one of our last nights in the big, old bed, and I am so glad. Squashed in between my two sisters, I feel like a jack-in-the-box, ready to pop out any second.

"How will she understand us?" Trudie asks. "She won't know any English."

"We'll have to teach her," Sophie says. "That's going to be my job, remember?"

"We can all help," I say quietly.

"Oh, of course," says Sophie. "I'm not sure how much time I'll have anyway. I'm very busy in school."

"I hope she doesn't bring too many things with her," Trudie says, looking around our small room. "It's already crowded enough in here." Shifting once more in the tightly packed bed, I have to agree with her. Still, I am eager for Tania's arrival.

"I hope she'll like dolls," I say. "Do you think she will?"

"Doesn't everyone like dolls?" Trudie says. She reaches down to touch her own doll, which is in a box on the floor just beside the bed. Even though Sophie and I have asked her a hundred times not to do this, she insists on keeping the box right there, where we are apt to stumble on it.

"We can show her the doll shop," I say. "I'll bet she'll

love it." I feel a pang when I remember that I had wanted to make Tania a doll but never got around to it. And the ideas I had before—the Russian princess, the Spanish dancer—somehow seem wrong to me now.

The next day drags by. I keep looking at the big clock that hangs on the front wall of my classroom. It seems to me that the slender black hands do not move at all but are frozen in place. History, geography, arithmetic . . . Will the lessons ever end? Our teacher, Miss Marsh, is not even here today. She is out sick, and we have a substitute. She is very young and giggles nervously when she has to give us instructions. I feel sorry for her.

Finally it is three o'clock, and as soon as we are dismissed, I race down the stairs in search of my sisters. We agreed that we would walk home as a group and greet Tania together. We don't stop to look at anything along the way, and even though today I have my allowance money in my pocket, I am not tempted for a second to stop for a root beer or penny candy.

But when we all clatter into the shop, we see Mama bent over her sewing machine and Papa at his desk, just like it's a normal day. There is no sign of Tania, no sign that today is different from yesterday or the day before.

"Where is she?" pants Trudie, dropping her satchel.

"She's still on Ellis Island," Mama says, turning to face us. "Papa went but he couldn't get her today."

"Why not?" I ask.

"There were so many people," Mama says. "Everything took much longer then we expected. But Papa will get her tomorrow."

"Oh," I say. I was so sure she'd be here by now.

"What's Ellis Island?" Trudie asks. "Is that where the lady with the torch stands?" Mama has told us about seeing the tall statue, Lady Liberty, from the boat.

"No, silly!" says Sophie. "The statue is on a different island. When you get to America, you have to pass through Ellis Island first."

"Did you have to go through Ellis Island, Mama?" Trudie wants to know.

Mama repositions the fabric under the needle of the sewing machine. "I did, and so did Papa, and so does almost everyone else who lands here."

"What do they do there?" asks Trudie.

"They ask a lot of questions. There are some forms to

fill out. A doctor examines you to make sure you don't have a contagious disease."

"What if you do?' Trudie wants to know. "Have a contagious disease, I mean."

"Sometimes the officials won't let you in," Mama says.

"What if that happens to Tania?" I ask. It would be terrible if after coming all that way she were not allowed into the country.

"It won't," Mama says firmly. But somehow, the way she says it makes me think she is trying to convince herself as much as she is trying to reassure me.

"Mama, is Tania all alone on Ellis Island?" Trudie asks. Her voice sounds a little frightened, which is just how I feel.

"No," Mama says. "She's not. Aunt Rivka's friend is with her."

Trudie sighs and clomps upstairs. I follow her. A whole night and day to wait. It seems like Tania will never, ever get here.

# 6

## SHANNON

Our room has been scoured in anticipation of Tania's arrival—furniture dusted and shined, floor mopped and waxed, curtains pressed and starched. And the new beds are here! Last week, Papa went uptown, to a furniture store on Fourteenth Street, and ordered two white, enameled iron bunk beds. This morning, just before we left for school, a scarlet truck with gold lettering on the side drove up to our building. All of our neighbors gathered round or poked their heads out of their windows to watch the deliverymen bring the new beds upstairs.

There are new mattresses on each bed, springy and firm, and new pillows, too. We still have our old blankets, but Mama sewed each of us a new coverlet to spread over the blanket during the day. Mine is red-and-white checks, Sophie's is gray-and-white checks and Trudie's is pink-and-white checks. But Mama ran out of checked material, so Tania's is just a pure, deep blue, the color I imagine her eyes will be.

I stretch out on the top bunk of my new bed, ready to settle in with my library book—it's about unicorns—when all of a sudden, a loud, rumbling sound erupts from my stomach.

"What was *that*?" Sophie says.

"I guess I'm a little hungry." I say.

"I guess so!" Sophie says.

At lunch today, I was so excited telling my friends Esther and Batya about Tania's arrival that I barely even touched my lunch. By the time I got around to eating it, the bell had rung and I had to scoot back to class. So now, starved, I climb down from my new bed and head to the kitchen. Dinner won't be ready for a while, so I fix myself a snack of bread and butter sprinkled with cinnamon sugar and pour a glass of milk. Sitting down at the table, I stub my toe on Trudie's satchel, so I lug it out of the way. It's so heavy. What does she keep in there anyway—lead weights?

I take a big bite of the bread. Just then I get an idea—it's a *brilliant* idea, too—about what kind of doll I will make. Gobbling my bread quickly, I rub my sugar-coated lips with the back of my hand. Good thing Mama is not here. She would scold me for not using a napkin. But I am in a hurry.

Still, I stop to cut off a teensy-tinsy slice of cheese for Ginger Cat. I am only supposed to use scraps, but I don't see any right now, and I want to leave something in her dish. Then I run downstairs, leave the cheese in the box outside, and step into the doll shop.

I find Mama bent over her machine, sewing a batch of doll clothes. Kathleen is attaching the caps to the heads of some Nurse Nora dolls. Her husband Michael is piling some boxes on a shelf, and Papa is at his desk, going over some figures on a pad. He's wearing his glasses and a small frown. Figures always make him a little cross. I know just how he feels—figures and arithmetic make me cross, too. "Did you need something?" Mama looks up from her sewing machine.

"I want to make a doll," I tell her.

"A doll?" she asks. "You mean one of our dolls—Nora or the fairy?"

"No," I say looking down. I had wanted this to be a surprise. But that's not possible. "I want to make a doll for Tania. As a present. She might not have a doll, you know."

"Why Anna, that's such a thoughtful idea," Mama says, smiling. "What sort of doll did you have in mind?"

"It's a secret. Do I have to tell?"

"Of course not," Mama says. "Just let us know if you need anything." She goes back to her sewing. I stand there for a minute, looking around for materials, parts, and supplies. I can use one of the bodies from Nurse Nora, and one of the faces, too. I just need some yarn for the hair . . . now where could it be? Didn't Papa used to keep all the yarn right on the shelf over there?

"Lookin' for something, darlin'?" says Kathleen. I turn. Kathleen has bright red hair and a whole face full of freckles. Her big, friendly eyes are round and amber. She and her husband Michael came over from Ireland. Sometimes, she tells me stories about her cottage back in an Irish village, and about the hard times long ago when the potato crops failed and people didn't have enough to eat. Like my parents and Tania, Kathleen and Michael made "the crossing." And like Tania, they spent time on Ellis Island.

"Is there a spare doll body and head I could use? And I need some yarn, too," I say.

"I think I can help with that," Kathleen says. I love listening to her. Her lilting accent makes everything sound like a song. She climbs on a stepladder and brings down a box of yarn. So that's where it's kept. Yellow, brown, black . . . But I choose a rich orangey-red, a color that's like Kathleen's hair. Then she pulls out a box of fabric scraps and another of odds and ends left over from the doll hospital days. "Can you use what's in here?" she asks.

"Yes. This is perfect." I peer into the box. "Thank you so much!" Kathleen goes back to attaching the dolls' caps. Michael finishes stacking the boxes and brings one of them to the door. He has black hair that stands up from his head like fur, and a beard covering his wide, jolly face.

"I'm steppin' out to deliver this now, Mr. Breittlemann," he says to Papa. Papa nods briefly and looks back down at the figures. Michael gives me a wink before hoisting the box in his strong arms and heading off.

I find a little open space on one of the tables and lay out my materials. I am going to make a schoolgirl doll. She won't be a fantasy or a fiction. She'll be a regular girl just like me. Or Tania.

Since I helped design and make the very first Nurse Nora, I have some idea about where to begin. I start by securing the orange wool to the doll's scalp, using glue and adding a few stitches, just to be sure it will stay put. Then I plait the yarn into two neat braids and tie the ends with snippets of black ribbon. I cut out the pieces for a simple costume: gray flannel jumper and white blouse. When I have sewn the pieces together by hand, I slip them on the doll and tie a bit of black velvet ribbon at the neck. That looks pretty.

"How are you farin'?" Kathleen asks. I look up to see

her standing in front of me. She's wearing her jacket and her hat.

"Are you going home?" I ask.

"It's five thirty," she says, glancing at the clock on the wall.

"I'm going to keep working," I tell her. I got so involved with making the doll that I lost track of the time.

"Good luck with your dolly," she says, and heads out the door.

"It's almost time for dinner," Mama says from where she sits by the machine.

"Just a little while longer," I plead.

"All right," Mama says. "But come up as soon as I call you." Mama turns off the machine, and Papa puts aside his figures. They go upstairs, and I am alone in the shop, except for Goldie, our pet canary. Canaries are the only pets Papa will allow. He says customers like their singing. We've had Goldie for years, but recently, Papa brought home a lady friend for him. Her name is Zahava, which means "Goldie" in Hebrew. My sisters and I think this is so funny: Mr. Goldie and Mrs. Goldie.

I look in the box Kathleen gave me. Inside I find a few leftover things from back when our shop was for repairing dolls, not making them—a pair of ribbed, white socks, and a pair of shiny, black shoes. The socks are just right, but the shoes are a bit too big. I stuff the toes with crumpled bits of paper. Now they fit fine.

I hold the doll up and away from me so I can inspect her. The braids are good, and so is the outfit. But it seems to me she needs something more, something that will make it clear that she is a schoolgirl and not just any girl.

At once, it hits me. A satchel. The doll should have a satchel, like the ones my sisters and I lug back and forth to and from school every day. A satchel carries books, of course. But it also carries a snack, a note from a friend, a test with a bright red A on top. Satchels carry a sweater, mittens, a forgotten lemon drop you are so happy to find. I wrapped Bernadette Louise in a towel and brought her to school in my satchel. Trudie's satchel is always filled to bursting. I remember how heavy it was when I stubbed my toe on it earlier today. The more I think about it, the more important the satchel seems. This doll *needs* a satchel. And it is up to me to make it.

"Anna! Dinner!" calls Mama. Dinner *now*? I just got the very best idea I have had all day.

"Coming," I call. I set the doll on the table. "I'll be back," I whisper. If I can talk to my own doll, I can talk to this one, too.

I bound up the stairs, shove my hands under the faucet, and sit down at the table. Mama is serving vegetable *kugel*, which is a noodle pudding, and patties that she made from leftover chicken. It's a meal I usually love, but tonight, I bolt the food down and beg to be allowed to return to my work downstairs.

"What are you doing anyway?" Sophie asks. "I haven't seen you all afternoon."

"It's a surprise," I tell her. "You'll see when it's done." I turn to my mother. "Please can I go back down, Mama? Just for a little while?"

"Are your lessons finished?" Papa asks.

"We don't have any!" I say happily. "Miss Marsh was out sick today and there was a substitute teacher. She didn't give us any work to take home."

"Well, if Mama says it's all right . . ." Papa says. I look over at Mama, who nods her head.

"Thank you!" I say. I get up and take my plate to the sink, where I wash it hastily. Then, it's back downstairs to the schoolgirl doll I have left on the table. Goldie and Zahava tweet briefly when I enter the shop but soon settle down.

I am still thinking of the satchel. But how will I make it? I rummage through the box again, and there, at the bottom, is a wadded-up bit of canvas. It's dull beige, almost the exact color of our satchels. Using Mama's iron, I press it smooth. Then I sketch a pattern onto the material. Cutting it is hard because the scissors are not strong enough. I keep at it, even though it hurts my hand. Soon, all the pieces are cut.

Sewing is hard, too. The first needle will not go through the fabric. I have to hunt all over to find a big, thick needle. Best of all is when I go through the box one more time and find a few twisted doll's belts with tiny gold-colored buckles. I pull the buckles off two of them and attach them to the flap of the satchel. Now it can be opened and closed, just like a real satchel.

The last thing I want to do is paint a few freckles across her nose, so I find the tubes of paint and a handful of brushes. Choosing a thick one for mixing, I create a color somewhere between orange and brown. Then, using the thinnest brush in the bunch, I dot tiny freckles on the doll's face. "Anna!" calls Mama. Her voice sounds just a smidgen irritated. "Anna, you need to get ready for bed."

"Just in time," I say to the doll. "Now all you need is a name." And as soon as I have said those words, the name comes to me: Shannon. Shannon is the name of an Irish river. Kathleen has a sister back in Ireland named for it. She's told me all about her.

"Anna!" Mama calls again. "Anna, I do mean now!"

"I'll be right there!" I call back. And grabbing Shannon the School Girl under my arm, I flip off all the lights and take the stairs two at a time.

# 7

## $\mathcal{W}$ELCOME, TANIA

The next day, I wake up early, before anyone else in the family. I'm just so excited about Tania's arrival. Quietly, I get dressed and remove Shannon from her hiding place under my pillow. I am just as pleased with the doll this morning as I was last night. Maybe even more. I look at her cheery freckles and pat her orangey-red hair and tuck her way back under the pillow before my sisters wake up. Even though Mama and Kathleen know about the doll, no one has actually seen her yet. I want Tania to be the first.

At school we have a special assembly during which a group of actors performs a play. It is Shakespeare's A

*Midsummer Night's Dream*, and it is set in a lush forest filled with fairies, spirits, and all kinds of magic. Later, during our geography lesson, we draw maps of Europe. Miss Marsh is back and says my map is so well done that she picks it as an example to show to the whole class. I took special care with drawing and coloring Russia, because that's where Tania was born. Even our arithmetic lesson is not too bad today. Miss Marsh has brought in several loaves of pound cakes that we have to divide into different fractional pieces. When the lesson is over, we get to eat the cake. It's delicious.

Three o'clock comes sooner than I expect. I meet my sisters right outside school, and once again, we race home after school. This time when we get there, Papa is gone—a good sign!—and Mama is in the shop with Kathleen and Michael. Today Michael is whistling while he stacks the boxes. He whistles better than anyone I have ever heard.

"How did the doll turn out?" Kathleen asks. I know she means to be kind, but I shake my head and whisper, "Not yet." She nods and doesn't say anything else about it. Fortunately, neither Sophie nor Trudie seems to have heard her question. Today Kathleen is working on a group of fairy dolls, which have wings made of wire and gauze that attach to their shoulders. She sews a few tiny sequins on each wing. They remind me of Titania, the beautiful queen of the fairies in the play we saw today.

"When will Papa be home?" Trudie asks.

"I don't know," Mama answers. She turns to Sophie. "Why don't you girls start your lessons? That way you'll have gotten some of them done before your cousin gets here." Sophie goes into the kitchen and Trudie follows. I'll go, too, but first I pause so I can say something to Kathleen.

"I promise I'll show you the doll later," I tell her. "But for now, I wanted it to be a surprise."

"No need to worry, darlin'," says Kathleen, head bent over her sewing. "I can keep a secret." The sequins wink in the light.

All of a sudden, Mama grabs a roll of muslin, holds it up, and frowns. "What—again?" she says. Kathleen, Michael, and I all look in her direction.

"What's wrong, Mama?" I ask.

"Mice!" exclaims Mama. "They get into everything." She holds up a roll of muslin that has been chewed at one end.

"Maybe Ginger Cat could help with the mice," I say.

"You know that Papa says cats are for outdoors," argues Mama. "He doesn't want a cat living inside the apartment."

"But they catch mice," I point out.

"That's true," she says. "And we need a mouse catcher. . . ."

She pauses, as if thinking. "Where is the cat now?"

"I'm not sure. But she's been coming by for food— the dish is always empty after we've filled it. Do you want to see?"

Together, we walk outside, and sure enough, there is nothing in the saucer. To my surprise, Ginger Cat is sitting in the box right next to it! She looks up at us very prettily, as if to say, "May I please have some more?"

"Hello kitty," I say extending my hand to pet her. She startles and darts off.

"Papa told you not to touch," Mama scolds. "It's a good thing she didn't scratch."

"I'm sorry, I forgot. Sitting there like that, she looked so tame."

"Well, you have to be careful just the same," says Mama. "You may not be so lucky next time."

"Anna, come quick! They're here!" Trudie's words interrupt Mama's lecture.

We hurry inside and upstairs, all thoughts of the cats forgotten for the moment. Finally, Tania has arrived. Standing in the kitchen is a slender, shy-looking girl of about my height. Mama rushes over and kisses her twice, once on each cheek. Then she says something to her in Yiddish, but Tania doesn't answer.

Mama turns to us. "Girls, meet your cousin Tania," she says in English. "Tania, this is Sophie. And that's Anna, and here is Trudie." She slips into Yiddish, and I am guessing she repeats her introductions so Tania can understand.

"Hello Tania," I say. Mama told us not to worry about speaking Yiddish. Tania will need to learn English, so we might as well just start right in. On impulse, I give her a big hug. But I feel her stiffen in my arms, so I let go. I look at her more closely then. She really does have blonde hair, just as I imagined she would. It's long and thick and would be beautiful were it not so . . . dirty. Her clothes are dirty, too, and I can see crescents of black underneath her fingernails. Well, it must have been hard to stay clean on the boat and Ellis Island, I think, defending her in my own mind. Now that's she here, she can have a hot bath, and Mama can wash her clothes.

I glance down at Tania's feet. She wears boots that are worn and broken. I can see her bare toes peeking out from the holes. Those boots will need more than simple cleaning. Her bag, a battered and worn-looking thing, sits on the floor right next to her. It is small. She has not brought very much with her. I look up, wanting to see her eyes. Are they as blue as I thought they would be? Yes, even more blue, but I only see them for a second. When she catches me looking at her, she quickly looks away.

"Do you want to see our room?" Trudie asks. Her voice is timid, as if she is a little afraid of Tania.

Tania doesn't say anything. Of course not. She can't understand. Mama repeats Trudie's question in Yiddish. Tania still doesn't answer. I want to take her hand to lead

her to the room. But after the way she reacted when I hugged her, I am reluctant.

"Don't worry, girls," Mama says. "Tania is just a little shy. She'll feel more comfortable soon." She turns to Tania and begins a low, steady stream of Yiddish. Tania doesn't say anything. She stands there and chews on one of her exceedingly dirty nails and blinks rapidly, as if the sun is shining in her eyes.

"Let's give Tania a snack," Mama says. "And then she can have a nice hot bath." Mama repeats this in Yiddish. I see Tania glance at the claw-footed bathtub and then glance away. I can't imagine that she will object. I never saw anyone who needed a bath so badly.

Mama leads Tania to the sink to wash her hands, and then to the table, where she sets out the fresh raisin cake she has baked for our cousin's arrival. Sophie, Trudie, and I each have a piece of cake and a tall glass of milk. Tania just looks at the piece Mama has put before her.

"Do. You. Want. Cake?" Sophie says clearly and slowly. She accompanies these words with a series of gestures. First she points to Tania, then to the cake, and finally to her mouth. She pretends to chew. Tania responds by blinking rapidly. I am beginning to see that this is a nervous habit she has. Sophie seems annoyed when Tania doesn't understand. But then, Sophie is annoyed by anyone who is not able to grasp things quickly.

"It's all right, girls," Mama says. "Tania will join you if she feels like it." We start eating our cake, which is so tasty that I ask for another slice. Mama says no, it will spoil my dinner. Tania finally breaks off a tiny piece and gnaws it. Trudie, Sophie, and I finish our cake, and Sophie brings the plates to the sink, where she washes them. Trudie reaches for her satchel. I feel a bit strange, sitting there and watching as Tania stares at her cake without finishing it. Finally, Mama asks me to get her sewing basket in the parlor. I am relieved to have a reason to get up from the table.

I return with the basket. Tania is not there. Neither is her piece of cake. Maybe she ate it after all. I am guessing she went into the bedroom, to get ready for her bath. The pots of water are heating up on the stove now, and because our tub is in the kitchen, Mama has set up the screen for privacy. Good. That hot bath will surely make

Tania feel better. And there's still Shannon, I think. Maybe Shannon will help.

I go into our room, where Sophie is curled up on her bed, copying something from her French book. She is studying French this year and makes a big show of telling us that *parler* means *to speak* and *marcher* means *to walk*. Trudie is sprawled on the floor, doing what looks like fifty arithmetic problems. I should start my own lessons, too. I have a composition to write and another map to complete. Before I get started, I go over to the bed that is Tania's and pretend to be fluffing the pillow. What I am really doing is making a space for Shannon. I have taken her out of her hiding place under my pillow and plan to put her under Tania's as a surprise. But when my hand moves around, I feel something crumbly and slightly sticky. I pull out a piece of Mama's raisin cake.

"Look," I say to my sisters, "I found this under Tania's pillow."

"It's a piece of raisin cake," Sophie says. "But how did it get *there*?"

"I know I didn't do it," I say to Sophie. "Did you?" Sophie shakes her head. We both look at Trudie.

"It wasn't me," she says.

"It must have been Tania," I say.

"Why in the world would she do that?" asks Trudie.

Neither Sophie nor I can think of a good reason for such a thing, and so the question remains unanswered.

A little while later, Tania comes in from her bath. My sisters and I stop what we are doing to look at her. Her long, gold hair has been washed and combed. Her cheeks are flushed from the hot water, and next to the pink, her eyes seem even bluer than before. She is wearing a clean, though ragged dress, and a pair of shoes that are only a little less worn than her boots. But her blinking, which I noticed earlier, is rapid and constant.

"I sleep in the bed above yours," I tell her. Tania just blinks. "We made some space for your things in the cupboard. . . ." Still more blinking. I look at my cousin and sigh. This is going to be harder than I thought. But then I remember Shannon.

"I have something for you," I say, pulling Shannon out from under the pillow. I take care not to move the piece of cake, and reach behind it instead. "It's a doll." I hand her to my cousin. "I made her for you."

At first, Tania just stares. But after a moment, she reaches out to touch Shannon's hair and then her face.

"Go on," I say. "She's yours now. You can take her." I am so glad to see Tania show some interest in something. I know she doesn't understand my words, but I hope that the sound of my voice will make my meaning clear. And it seems to work. She reaches for the doll.

"You made her?" Sophie says as she watches Tania

with Shannon. "Is that what you were up to all day yesterday?"

I nod, watching Tania with the doll. She must like her if she's holding her so tightly, right? And yet she doesn't smile. Instead, she has a sad, almost desperate look on her face. And she is holding the doll as if she expects someone to take it away from her.

"She's darling!" exclaims Trudie. "I love her little satchel. Does it open?" Trudie doesn't seem to notice Tania's odd reaction.

"It does," I say to Trudie. But my eyes remain on Tania, who presses her face against Shannon's hair. Tania's lips quiver, and from her closed eyes, I see tears slowly begin to trickle down her face.

"Tania's crying," Trudie says, staring at our cousin.

"Maybe she's tired. Or homesick," Sophie says. She seems puzzled, too.

"Maybe," I say. But somehow I don't think that's the reason. Or not all of it anyway. No, I think Tania is crying because she can't believe the doll is really hers. Maybe she is not used to receiving something so nice.

"Should we tell Mama?" Trudie asks. Sophie and I look at each other, trying to decide. It turns out we don't have to. With a very loud *sniff*, Tania dries her tears on her sleeve and stops crying. Then she turns to go into the kitchen, still holding Shannon as if she will never let her go.

# 8

## ℱIRST DAY

The next day, Mama walks to school with us. She wants to make sure that Tania is able to find her classroom, and she wants to introduce Tania to the teacher. After all, going to school is part of the reason Tania came all the way from Russia to America.

"Will Tania be in my class?" I ask Mama. I look over at my cousin. Her hair, long, thick, and butter blonde, has been brushed until it gleams, and then plaited by Mama into a pair of heavy braids. I have always envied Sophie's shiny brown hair, which today is tied back with a checked grosgrain ribbon, but I have a hunch even Sophie would agree that Tania's hair is prettier.

"I know you would like that, but no, she'll need to be with younger children for a while," Mama replies.

"What about my class?" Trudie asks. "I'm younger."

"No, I'm afraid that won't be the right class either," Mama says.

"So what class will she be in?" I ask.

"She'll be in with the first graders," Mama says. "The little ones who are just learning to read."

First grade! I think. Six-year-olds. I would hate that. Will Tania? I glance in her direction. She is wearing a plaid dress that Mama made for me, and shoes that were once Sophie's. When Mama helped Tania unpack, it was clear that many of her things would need to be thrown away. They were so worn out. Mama will wash what she kept, but until everything is clean, dry, and pressed, Tania will borrow from me. I don't mind. I think the dress looks nice on her. Tania also has a new satchel that Mama must have bought for her.

We are almost at the school now. Boys and girls from all grades are heading in the same direction. They are talking and laughing, grabbing at each other's hats and yanking on each other's satchels. I see my friends Esther and Batya across the street, and we wave to each other. Esther runs over to join us.

"Is this your cousin?" she asks. Esther knows all about Tania. I've been talking about her for weeks.

"It is," I say. "Do you want to meet her?"

"Oh, yes!" says Esther.

"This is Esther," I say to Tania. She does that blinking thing with her eyes. I have to admit, it is starting to bother me.

"Hello, Tania," says Esther with a big smile. "I hope you like our school."

Tania says nothing.

"She doesn't understand English yet," I tell Esther. Esther repeats what she has said in Yiddish. Esther's parents don't speak English at all, so Esther speaks Yiddish at home. But Tania still says nothing.

Esther looks at me questioningly. "I guess your cousin is kind of . . . shy," she says finally.

"She is," I say. "But we're hoping she'll get over it soon."

I part company with my mother, sisters, and cousin at the front doors to the school. Trudie heads off to fourth grade, Sophie to eighth. I head off to my own sixth-grade class. And Tania walks down the hall with Mama, in the direction of the first-grade classroom.

All morning long, I think of my cousin in with the six-year-olds. Finally, the bell rings for lunch. Esther, Batya, and I usually stand in line to buy our lunch, and then sit together. I'll ask Tania to join us. But Tania is not in the lunchroom. "Wait for me here?" I ask Esther, who nods. I go up to the first-grade classroom. No Tania. On my way back down, I find her standing alone, outside the lunchroom door.

"Time to eat," I tell her. I am not surprised when her only reply is the blinking of her long feathery lashes. But this time, I am bolder and take her hand. She flinches a little but lets me lead her inside, where Esther and Batya are waiting. Esther keeps up a steady stream of chatter in both English and Yiddish. Tania nods and shakes her head a few times, but she doesn't speak. And she doesn't really eat either.

I think of the raisin cake, tucked beneath her pillow. Sophie, Trudie, and I agreed that we wouldn't tell Mama and Papa. We don't want to tattle.

Right now, Tania eats a slice of carrot, a forkful of rice. But when we get up to leave, I see her stuff the pockets of the plaid dress with two uneaten rolls. Esther sees it, too.

"I think your cousin is a little strange," she says to me in a low voice. "She's not eating her food. But she's staring at it."

"I know," I say, feeling a pang of disloyalty. I am well aware that Tania does not seem to want to eat in front of anyone. She wants to take the food away, to eat later or to hide. But I don't want to say all this to Esther, at least not yet, so I quickly change the subject.

At the end of the day, I meet my sisters and Tania. We all start out for home. Sophie walks ahead. At lunch, Sophie sat at a table with some of her eighth-grade friends. I saw how she glanced in our direction and then looked away again quickly. It was clear she did not want to be associated with Tania, at least not while she was at school.

I look over at Tania, trying to sneak a look at her

pockets without seeming too obvious. Has she eaten either of the rolls she took from lunch? Her pockets don't bulge, so maybe she did. I hope so.

After our lessons—Mama helps Tania with hers—and a supper of meat dumplings, green beans, and roasted potatoes, we give Tania a tour of the shop. We point out where the supplies like buckram, muslin, and skeins of wool are kept and show her the different dolls. Tania, still holding Shannon, expresses no interest at all. So we decide to hold a "fashion show" for our own dolls instead. Tania can be the audience.

Each of our dolls will "model" some of the outfits we have made for her. I have to admit that Sophie's are the best. Using scraps Mama has given her, Sophie has sewn a chiffon dress, a velvet walking suit, a summer dress of lilac-colored linen, and a brocade evening skirt with a matching jacket. Her stitches are so tiny and fine.

We clear off a worktable so we have plenty of room. Trudie is the "dresser" and gets the dolls ready. Sophie and I take turns moving them down the length of the table, and Sophie provides a running commentary. When it is her doll's turn she says, "Victoria Marie wears a summery chiffon dress in a delicate shade of the palest pink. Note the ruffles on the skirt; they look like petals. Heads will turn at the ball when she appears in this stunning design." I think Sophie is so clever.

Tania watches and listens without seeming to enjoy any of it. Even if she can't understand the words, surely the dolls ought to intrigue her. But she is only interested in Shannon. While Sophie is talking, she plays with the doll's hair and fiddles with her clothing. She opens and closes the buckles on the satchel. She takes off her shoes and socks and puts them back on again. Finally, Sophie stops talking.

"Can I see that doll?" she asks.

Tania looks horrified. She holds the doll more tightly than ever.

"I'll give her right back," Sophie says.

Still Tania holds on.

"Maybe Mama can explain to her that you just want to look at the doll, not take it away from her," I say.

"Oh, let her keep her old doll," Sophie says. "I don't really want to see it anyway."

"Well, I'd like to see it," Trudie says. "I want to see her clothes better. And her freckles, too. You did such a good job, Anna! Have you shown her to Papa?"

"Not yet," I say. I'm glad Trudie likes Shannon, but I wish Tania could share, even for a little while.

We put everything away and are ready to go upstairs when Trudie asks, "What about the cats?" Sophie and I both look at her. "Tania isn't interested in our dolls. But maybe she'll be interested in Ginger Cat and Plucky."

"You could be right," Sophie says. She turns to Tania. "Do you like cats?" she asks. When Tania doesn't answer, Sophie drops down on the floor and actually pretends to *be* a cat. She arches her back, and lets out a very convincing "meow." To my utter surprise, Tania smiles, a small, kind of broken-looking smile.

"Come on then!" Trudie says. "Let's go." Together, we go out in the yard to inspect the box. Ginger Cat is sitting in it, waiting by the empty saucer. Tania stares at her, blinking furiously. Then she cautiously approaches the cat.

"Careful, she might scratch," I warn. I pretend to

scratch my own arm, so Tania will understand. But Ginger Cat neither bolts nor scratches. Instead, she allows Tania to approach her and even sits still for a second while Tania touches her head very gently. Then the cat opens her mouth in a soft meow.

"She likes Tania," Trudie says. Tania picks up the empty saucer and takes it inside and upstairs. We trail behind, curious. She hands it to Mama and says something in Yiddish. Mama nods and goes over to the icebox. She takes out a bit of leftover gefilte fish and puts it in the saucer. We follow Tania as she brings the dish downstairs and sets it in the box. Ginger Cat is still there, and she meows again. But this time, it sounds like she is saying "thank you," before she bends her head and begins to eat.

When we are getting ready for bed, I watch as Tania undoes her braids and brushes out her lustrous golden hair. She sets Shannon on the bed and adjusts her skirt. Well, she likes the doll and she likes Ginger Cat. It's a start. And I have to tell her about Plucky. Tania will certainly want to know about him. Maybe Esther can help me.

But when Tania leaves the room, I find myself noticing that her pillow looks lumpy. Even though I shouldn't, I peek underneath. When I do, I see two pieces of bread, a turnip, and a partially eaten bagel. Tania is storing food under her pillow. And something tells me she's not going to stop.

# 9

## MOUSE IN THE HOUSE

"Look," I say to Sophie when I am sure Tania is in the other room. "More food under the pillow."

"I think we have to tell Mama," Sophie says. "Not eating at the table and hiding the food away is such a strange thing to do. And besides, it's not sanitary!"

Sophie does have a point. But I want Tania to like and trust me. If I tell on her, that's not going to happen.

"Maybe," I say to Sophie. "But isn't it like tattling?"

"Tattling is when you are telling to be mean," Trudie says. "You would be telling because you want help her." Is this really my little sister saying these words? She sounds so grown up and so wise.

"Trudie is right, Anna," says Sophie. "I'm going to tell Mama now."

"Please don't!" I beg. "Wait just a little longer. Maybe I can figure out how to fix things without telling Mama and Papa. Or maybe she'll stop on her own."

"All right," Sophie grumbles. "But don't wait too long, or I'm telling Mama. I don't like having food stuffed under the pillow in our room. And I don't like *her*."

"Sophie! She's our cousin. She's lonely and sad. Can't you understand that?"

"I know, and I'm sorry for her. But being sorry for someone and liking her are not the same thing."

"She kind of scares me," Trudie confesses. "Sometimes she seems all right, but other times, she's kind of strange. The first graders think so, too."

"Who told you that?" It upsets me to think that other children have been talking about Tania. Do they tease her? I hope not.

"My friend Frieda has a sister in that class," Trudie says. "She says Tania won't look at anyone, even the teacher. And that she hides food in her desk."

So she's doing it at school, too. "I still think she'll change," I say stubbornly. "We have to give her a chance." But neither Sophie nor Trudie looks like they believe me.

Several days later, Papa pokes his head out of the shop when I return home from school. "Anna, can I talk to you for a minute?" I join him at his desk at the far end of the workspace where he goes over all the bills, figures, and money.

"It's about that doll you made," he begins, picking up a pencil and twirling it between his fingers. "The one Tania won't let go of."

"That's Shannon," I say. "She's a schoolgirl."

"What gave you the idea?" Papa asks.

"Well, at first I thought I would make a Russian princess. Because Tania is Russian." Papa nods in an interested way, so I go on. "I also thought about a Spanish dancer, because I liked the costume—the black lace shawl and the fan." Papa smiles at that. "But in the end, I wanted to make a doll that was more real. A doll that was a friend. Not a fantasy."

"Yes, yes I see your point," Papa says, looking more excited by the minute. "The simple costume, the book bag. Now *that's* a really original touch. Here's a doll that will reflect a little girl's own life." The next time I see Mr. Greenfield at F.A.O. Schwarz, I want to show her to him. How do you feel about that?"

How do I feel about that? I am thrilled. Just thrilled. But then I think about Tania. Will she let her doll go long enough for Mr. Greenfield to see it? Maybe Papa can explain it to her. I hope so.

Although we have not discussed it, Tania has taken over the job of leaving food out for Ginger Cat, who seems to grow tamer by the day. Esther helped me tell Tania about Plucky, and she's eager to see him, too. That evening, I bring Tania up to the roof, so we can look for Plucky from there. He's about a month old, and his fur, now fuller and a creamy apricot, will be visible from up above. We have to wait, but soon we spot him, hopping along on three legs. The useless hind paw that dangled from his leg is no longer there. It must have fallen off, just like Papa said.

As soon as she sees him, Tania grabs my hand and starts jabbering away in Yiddish. Her whole face is different, her eyes brighter, her smile wide. I wish I could understand what she is saying, but whatever it is, I can see that she has fallen in love with him already. Well, who *wouldn't* love Plucky?

Despite his having only three legs, he seems very spry. He's just a little thin, that's all. But his fur, even from this distance, seems dull. A bit matted, too. Is he getting enough to eat? I don't think so. It's already October. Today there is a slight chill in the air, and the afternoon sunlight is fading quickly. Soon it will be winter. What will happen to Plucky then?

I look at Tania again. She is still gazing at Plucky. Does she know that he may be in danger? I have to talk to Papa, I decide. Right away. I take Tania's hand to lead her down with me. It is clear that she does not want to follow me. She plants herself on the roof and points to Plucky.

"I know you want to watch him some more," I tell her. "But he's looking too *thin. Underfed.* Maybe he has a *disease.* We have to tell Papa." I point to Plucky and close my eyes, moaning, like I am sick. That seems to get through, because she willingly follows me downstairs.

I expect to find Papa in the shop, but he is in the

apartment. In our room, in fact. He looks upset about something. Quite upset.

"Where was it?" he asks Trudie and Sophie, who are both sitting on their beds with their feet drawn up tightly under them. "Show me exactly where you saw it."

"It was right there, Papa," Trudie says, pointing. "It was just a little bitty thing. Gray, with a long tail. I don't think it would hurt anyone. But it did scare me. It was so fast!"

"What was so fast?" I say, looking from my sister to my father. Though I think I already know.

"A mouse!" says Trudie. "In our room!"

"First downstairs, now up here . . ." mutters Papa.

My heart starts beating very fast. If there are mice in our room, I have a good idea why. It must be because of the food that Tania has been hiding.

"It's because of her!" Sophie cries, pointing at our cousin. "She's been hiding food in her bed! She does it at school, too. All the kids know."

I look at Sophie, horrified. Surely Tania does not understand the words. But the tone, the look, the accusing finger—those are the same in any language.

"What's all the yelling about?" Mama comes into the room.

"Trudie and Sophie saw a mouse," Papa explains. "And Sophie says it's because Tania has been hiding food under her pillow."

Mama looks from Sophie's angry face to Tania's frightened one. She begins talking to Tania in Yiddish, and her gentle tone makes Tania's expression relax just a little. Then Mama takes Tania's hand and leads her to the bed. She motions for Tania to move the pillow aside, and with great reluctance, Tania does as she is asked. Silently, we all stare at the three hard-boiled eggs, raw potato, and two ginger snaps that Mama baked the other day, one with a bite taken out of it.

"So what if she is hiding food?" I burst out, unable to keep still a second longer. "Is that such a crime?"

"No," Papa says. "But we can't let it continue."

Mama starts talking to Tania in Yiddish again. Tania looks down at the floor, fists clenched, nodding and blinking. Shannon is jammed under her arm. When Mama is finished, Tania places Shannon on her bed, cups her hands over Mama's ear and starts whispering. Finally she stops.

Mama turns to the rest of us. "Things are very bad in Russia, even worse than when Papa and I lived there. The war is still going on. Jobs are scarce, and so is food. Aunt Rivka has been selling off furniture and the few pieces of Bubbe's jewelry that she has left. Some days she and Tania ate just one meal. Other days, they didn't eat at all." We all turn to Tania. But Tania grabs Shannon and bolts from the room. I hear her footsteps clattering down the stairs. Mama hurries after her.

"Mama will calm her down," Papa says, looking at us. "You girls have to understand how hard it is for her." He gives Sophie a pointed look, but Sophie doesn't seem bothered at all.

"We still have mice," is all she says. "What are we going to do about that?"

"What about using Ginger Cat and Plucky to help with the mice?" I ask.

"You mean the cats living outside?" Papa asks. I nod my head eagerly. "I told you: no cats indoors."

"What if she can help solve our mouse problem?" I say.

He seems to be thinking it over. "The mother cat might be a possibility. She seems tamer lately."

"She *is* tamer! And it's because of Tania, Papa. She just has a way with Ginger Cat. With all animals, I guess."

And at just that moment, Mama comes back into the room with her arm around Tania. I look over at my cousin. The awful blinking has slowed a little. I guess Mama knew what to say.

"Well, we can give it a try. But she'll have to earn her keep," says Papa.

"Hurray!" cries Trudie, jumping off of the bed to do what she calls her "happy dance," which consists of prancing in place, shaking her head from side to side, and making a circling motion with her hands. Even Sophie looks pleased, in her big-girl sort of way.

"What about Plucky?" I ask. "He could help with the mice, too."

"Not with that bad back leg," Papa says. "He won't be fast enough."

"Couldn't we keep him anyway, Papa? Please?" I beg. "He's gotten thin and his fur is all matted. What will happen when winter comes?" My eyes fill with tears.

"I know you care about him, *tochter*," says Papa. "It shows what a kind heart you have. But two cats are too many." He puts an arm around me. "You and Tania can toss scraps over the fence," he adds. "Plucky's a sturdy kitten. He'll be all right."

"What if he's not?" But Papa is gone. I turn to Mama. "Can you talk to him?" I ask. "Get him to change his mind?"

"Two cats are too many," Mama repeats. She gathers all the food that was under the pillow and leaves the room.

I look around to see my sisters still sitting on their beds, but Tania is no longer there. I didn't even see her go.

"Did you have to be so mean?" I ask Sophie

"I wasn't mean," Sophie says. "We have mice. Someone had to do something about it. And I could see it wasn't going to be you."

"But she went hungry, Sophie! When have we ever had to go hungry?"

"I told you before," Sophie says. "I feel very sorry for her. She's had a hard time. But things are not so hard now." Since Sophie is wearing her hair down today, with only a thin maroon headband securing it, she does that hair-tossing thing she likes to do. "Besides," she adds, "it's not like I got her in trouble. Mama and Papa weren't even angry."

"I know," I say. "But you made her think you don't like her."

"I don't," Sophie says calmly.

"How can you say that?" I cry. "Especially after what we just heard?"

"When you're as old as I am, you'll understand." She tosses her hair—again.

If getting older means being as cold and unfeeling as Sophie is right now, then I hope I stay eleven forever and ever.

# IO

## 𝒯HE OTHER SIDE OF THE FENCE

Over the next months, it is clear that while my sisters and my cousin are not exactly enemies, they are not friends either. Sophie avoids Tania. It's as if she is not there. And Trudie seems to follow Sophie's lead. They seem to have given up on Tania. But I haven't. And neither should they. Do they know that she is an excellent seamstress? Mama gives her some mending to help with, and her work is *perfect*. And when I look at her notebooks, I see the most wonderful doodles. She draws trees and houses and faces. But she mostly fills the margins of her notebook with horses, cows, rabbits, dogs, wolves, and of course cats, which seem to be her favorite. There is so much to like about Tania. I wish my sisters could see it.

But even Sophie has to grudgingly admit that Tania has a special way with animals. Thanks to Tania, Ginger Cat has become tame enough in these last few weeks to be considered our pet. While we have not actually seen her catch a mouse, we have no more little gray visitors, either upstairs or down, so we can assume that she is doing her job. She sleeps in the kitchen, on a cushion Tania has sewn for her, and every morning and evening, Tania faithfully sets out her dish of table scraps and her bowl of fresh water. Ginger Cat, now sleek and satisfied, allows herself to be stroked and scratched by all of us, though Tania is her clear favorite.

But if Ginger Cat is thriving, Plucky is not. From my rooftop perch, I can see that he looks even thinner and more matted. The days are short now, and the weather is cold. If Plucky is not well, he won't make it through the winter.

One early December day I notice something else even more troubling. There are trails of what look like white powder all along the edges of the yard on the other side of the fence, the yard where I have seen Plucky roaming. At first I think it is snow. But snow would not fall in such a neat, boxlike pattern. It has to be something else.

I look up at the fire escape where Plucky was born. The window is shut tightly, and a curtain hides whatever is going on inside. I think of the man with the mustache and his cruel broom. Does he have something to do with the white powder?

I don't want to ask Papa, since he will tell me to stay away from Plucky. I would ask Tania, but even though she seems to understand a few words, I still can't talk to her. Since I need advice *now*, I ask Sophie to come up to the roof with me. The wind blows our hair around our faces and seems to go right through my coat.

"There," I say, pointing to the white trail that snakes around the yard's edges. "Can you see it?"

"I can see it, but I wish I didn't," says Sophie grimly. "Anna, that powder is poison. If Plucky eats it, he'll die."

"Poison!" I exclaim. "How do you know?"

"I've seen it before. People sprinkle it in lines like that to kill rats. Papa told me about it."

"Are there rats in that yard?" I ask.

"Maybe," says Sophie. "Or it could be that someone is putting it down for Plucky." Sophie doesn't need to say who that someone is. We both know perfectly well. If I had thought the mustache man was evil before, I don't even know what to think of him now.

"I'm going to get Plucky and bring him here," I say firmly.

"Anna, you can't!" says Sophie. "Papa said not to."

"When he finds out about the poison, he'll change his mind," I say. "Besides, we have to rescue Plucky. We have to!"

Sophie and I go downstairs. When we get to the door of our apartment, she turns to me. "You're brave," she says softly.

"I haven't done anything yet," I say.

"Oh, yes you have," she says, and then slips back inside.

Late that night, after my sisters and Tania are asleep, I am still awake, staring up at the ceiling. The new bed is cozy and comfortable, but it's no use—I can't get to sleep. Finally, I get up and reach for Bernadette Louise who is seated on a shelf Papa hung over my bed. I know she can't hear me or talk, but it still helps me to pretend that she can. "What do you think I should do, Bernadette Louise?" I whisper.

She is wearing a flannel nightdress I made for her just this past week. I used a bit of the same blue flannel that we used to line the box for Ginger Cat, and added a snippet of lace to the hem. I want her to be warm. Just today I saw how the streets were lined with full, fragrant pines all ready to go home and take their place as Christmas trees in parlors and in sitting rooms all over the neighborhood. Mama has already brought out the brass menorah we use at Chanukah. It will be my job to polish it until it shines like gold.

I carry Bernadette Louise over to the window and look out. Our bedroom window faces the back, and though it is dark, my eyes soon adjust. I can see the traces of powder in the yard. And then, I detect a slight movement. It is Plucky, hopping along. He moves closer to a trail of powder, and then closer still.

*Don't!* I want to call to him. *Plucky, stay away!* I see him sniff delicately, and my heart is ready to burst out of my chest. *Please, please, please,* I pray. I cup my hand around the smooth, glazed surface of Bernadette Louise's head. I almost believe she is trying to tell me something. Suddenly, I know what it is. I put her on my pillow and draw the covers up around her. Then, trying not to make a sound, I climb down, take my shoes from their spot under the bed and tiptoe to the hall. My coat is hanging on a hook. I slip into it and hope that the opening and closing of the door won't wake anyone up.

*C·R·E·A·K!* The noise is so loud I am sure it will cause Papa and Mama to come running. I wait, hand frozen on the knob, to be discovered. But seconds pass and nothing happens. I close the door as quietly as I can and rush down the stairs and through the shop, where all the completed Nurse Noras lie side by side in their pale green boxes. The clock on the wall says it is 1:45. I am not sure if I have ever been up this late before.

Outside, the night is cold and clear. I hurry to the wall and begin my climb up and over. I have never scaled a wall this high before, and it is harder than I imagined.

At first, I can't get a proper grip but I keep trying, because I know Plucky is on the other side. Finally, I hoist myself up, scraping my hands and my knees. Once I am at the top, there is no turning back. I brace myself, look down at the ground on the other side, and jump. *Oooph!* I land with a little thud. My ankle hurts now, too. "Pssst," I call softly. "Plucky! Here boy!" I don't expect him to come, but I was smart enough to grab a bit of pot roast that was in Ginger Cat's dish. I hope Plucky will smell it and come close enough for me to catch him. For a few minutes, I stumble around on my sore ankle. I don't see him right away but then, after a bit, I can make out a small, furred shape hunched in a corner, behind some bags of trash.

"Plucky!" I whisper. "Are you hungry?" I extend my hand, which is a bit greasy by now. Very cautiously, Plucky rises up and begins to move toward me, his delicate head bobbing on his slim neck. He stops. He wants the food, but he is afraid. So I set it down on the ground, wipe my hand on my coat (hoping Mama won't notice the stain later), and wait.

He watches me with his round, golden cat's eyes as he

moves closer still. Then he bends down his head to eat.
As soon as he does, I am on him in a flash. He writhes
in my grasp, but I hold tight, even when his sharp little
claws take a swipe at my face. I feel a slice of pain, and I
am sure there is blood. But I still don't let go. Limping to
the wall, I try to scale it again, still keeping Plucky firmly
under my arm.

But once at the wall, I realize I have a big problem. It
was hard enough to scale the bricks the first time. Now
I am holding a squirming, scratching cat, and everything
hurts—palms, ankle, knees, cheek. As if all this is not
bad enough, Plucky begins to meow—loudly—in protest.

Suddenly, a light goes on upstairs and a window is
thrown open. I look up, horrified, to see the angry face of
the man with the mustache. "What are doing there?" he
shouts. "You're trespassing! I'll have you arrested!"

I want to run, but there is no place for me to go. I
can't scale the wall, the door into the building is locked,
and there is no access to the street or the other yards un-
less I climb another fence or wall, both of which I am unable to do. The man with the mustache disappears from
the window. I can hear his feet stomping down the stairs.

Another light goes on our building, and a head emerges from a window. Papa!

"What's all the commotion?" he calls. "People are trying to sleep!" More lights come on in the neighboring buildings, and more people come to their windows. Plucky wails piteously, twisting under my grasp.

"Papa!" I cry. "Papa, it's me, Anna! Come save me, Papa! Please!"

Just then, the door in the building leading to the yard bursts open, and there stands the man with the mustache. I am terrified.

"Wait right there!" Papa yells back. "I'm coming!"

"Who are you?" the man with the mustache yells, just as Plucky performs a sudden and final twist. He breaks free and leaps out of my arms onto his three legs. Hobbling as quickly as he can, he manages to disappear like an apricot-colored streak into the night.

I hear noises coming from our side of the wall, and there is Papa, climbing over and dropping down onto the hard, packed dirt. I have never been so glad to see him in my whole life.

# 11

## WHERE IS PLUCKY?

"Hold still," Mama says sternly. I wince when she touches me with the cotton ball. "It's for your own good." It is an hour later, and she is painting my cheek with gentian violet to prevent infection. She has already put it on my knees and hands. It burns. I must look silly with bright purple patches all over. But I don't feel like laughing.

Papa is pacing angrily back and forth as Mama cleans my wounds. "What were you thinking?" he says. "Don't you see how dangerous that was?"

I hang my head. But even though Papa is punishing me by taking away my allowance for a whole month, I am still glad he rescued me. As soon as he showed up,

I ran straight into his arms and told him everything. The man with the mustache was still yelling.

"Breaking and entering!" he hollered. "I'll have the police over here in five minutes!"

"Don't be ridiculous," Papa said. "She wasn't trying to steal from you. She was just trying to rescue the poor kitten. What kind of person puts poison out for a *kitten*?"

"I don't want that animal on my property," said the man. "Who knows what kind of disease he could be carrying?" He shook his head in disgust. "If you want him so badly, why don't you take him?"

Which, of course, was just what I was trying to do. Yet once Papa had calmed the man down, and the yelling turned to grumbling, Plucky was nowhere to be found.

Now, I am upstairs at the table, with Mama painting my hands and face, and my sisters and cousin goggle-eyed with all the excitement. There won't be much sleep for any of us tonight.

"Does it hurt?" Trudie asks. She sounds so concerned.

"Not too much," I say, wanting to reassure her.

"I told you you were brave!" exclaims Sophie when Mama is out of earshot. "I never would have had the nerve to try to rescue him."

"Tried and failed," I say. "Poor Plucky."

"Poor Plucky," repeats Tania. I look at her, amazed. Trudie's hands fly to her mouth, and even Sophie looks surprised. I have heard Tania say a few English words here and there, mostly to Mama. But these are the first words she has said directly to any of us. Never mind that what she said sounded more like "*Puhr Pluck-hee.*" I smile a big smile even though it makes my face hurt.

Finally, Mama finishes cleaning my cuts and scratches. "Now you girls have to get to bed!" she says. "We all need some sleep."

"But what about Plucky?" I ask. "Shouldn't we try to find him?"

"No!" Papa says sharply. "Not now, and not tomorrow. That cat is a menace. Stay away from him."

"That's not true," I plead. "He's not a bad cat, Papa. He was just scared. Especially when that horrible man showed up. You said it yourself, Papa. What kind of person tries to poison a kitten?"

"He's a terrible man," Papa says. "But I still won't allow the cat anywhere near you girls. If I find him, I'll have to take him away."

"Away? Where is away?" I ask. Papa does not answer.

"That's enough talk about cats for one night," Mama says, getting up from the table. She closes the bottle of gentian violet tightly. "To bed with all of you—now!"

A week goes by. Still no sign of Plucky. I wonder if Ginger Cat misses him as much as I do. Do cats miss each other? Maybe not, because Ginger Cat seems happy. She purrs when she sees Tania, who speaks to her in what sounds like a mix of Yiddish and English. "*Gut katz*," she says as she strokes Ginger Cat's head.

Ginger Cat has even taken to jumping in Papa's lap while he reads the newspaper at night. I think he likes it, because he gives her a little scratch behind the ears while she is sitting there. As for Plucky, I try to console myself by imagining that he has been found by another girl, one who will love him, if not as much as I do, then almost as much—which would be pretty good.

One night about a week after Plucky has disappeared, I am lying in bed just before lights out, when I start to cry. I just miss that little cat so much. Not wanting anyone to see me, I turn my face to the pillow. But that doesn't fool Trudie, who climbs up to the top bunk to sit next to me.

"Why are you so sad, Anna?" she asks.

"It's Plucky!" I say, lifting my face from the soggy pillowcase. "I wish he would come back!"

"Maybe he will," Sophie says. "You never can tell."

Tania pokes her head out of her bed and looks up at me. She is clutching Shannon and blinking in that way she still does sometimes, though thankfully not so much. Then she gets up, kneels down, and pulls a box out from under her bed. Curious, I lean over so I can see. Inside are the dove gray envelopes that must contain the letters she gets from her mother. But there are drawings in there, too, a whole bunch of them. She selects one and hands it to me. It's a picture of a small orange cat, curled up on a footstool. Plucky!

"Did you do that?" Trudie says, peering over my shoulder so she can see, too.

Shyly, Tania nods. She must have used the colored pencils Mama keeps in the shop.

"It's really good!" says Trudie.

"It's beautiful," I say, and hand the drawing back. And it is. Even more than his ears and his paws, his tail and his whiskers, she has captured something else about

Plucky. Something that seems to live *inside* him, not just on the outside.

Tania pushes the drawing back in my direction. She must want me to keep it. A present.

"Thank you," I tell her, taking the drawing once again.

Tania smiles shyly.

"Can I see?" Sophie asks. She has gotten out of her bed and is reaching up for the drawing. I am surprised. Since that night months ago when she tattled on Tania about the food, she has pretty much ignored our cousin. And Tania has kept her distance, too. Silently, I hand Sophie the drawing. She looks at it for a long time.

"This is the best drawing of a cat I have ever seen," she says finally. "It's so good it could be in a book. Or maybe even a museum." She hands the drawing back to me. I am not sure whether Tania understood everything that Sophie said, but her face has a gone a deep, pleased-looking pink. Then she does something else surprising. She hands Shannon to Sophie.

"You want to show her to me?" says Sophie. Tania nods, so Sophie takes Shannon and looks her over admiringly before handing her back. "She's a very special doll," Sophie says.

Soon it is the first night of Chanukah. We light candles in the menorah at sundown, and the smell of Mama's crispy brown latkes and cinnamon-laced applesauce is in the air.

There are small gifts for us to share, too, like a bag of almonds, an orange and, best of all, pieces of chocolate Chanukah gelt, wrapped in shining gold foil.

We use the gelt as part of the game we play with the wooden dreidel that always comes out of cupboard on the holiday. It's a game of chance that involves winning and losing the chocolate coins. First Sophie is winning, then Trudie, and finally Tania. But when we are done, we divide up the gelt again, so everyone gets the same number of pieces. I eat two of mine right away but decide to save the rest. I'll be glad have some left for tomorrow.

Later, Papa comes in to say good night. He sits down on Trudie's bed, and starts telling us the story of Chanukah. We all know it of course. But it's fun to lie in bed and listen to Papa tell it again. *A long, long time ago,* Papa begins, *the holy temple in Jerusalem was destroyed and the eternal flame was in danger of going out.* Papa explains how the flame had to remain lit all the time. The Jews of that time knew that they needed eight days to make more purified oil. There was only enough oil left in the lamp for a single night. But the oil miraculously burned for eight nights, long enough for new oil to be pressed and the lamp to be filled. So now we celebrate those eight nights by lighting candles to remember the miracle. As Papa talks, my mind drifts. Maybe there is room for a little miracle in our lives. Maybe Plucky will come back, safe and unharmed, and Papa will let him stay. Now wouldn't *that* be a miracle? I cannot help wishing.

⁓⁓⁓

Once Chanukah is over, Papa, Mama, and the O'Learys really have to buckle down to work. There's not much time until Christmas, and there are still plenty of dolls to prepare. Night after night, the four of them stay late in the doll shop, cutting, stuffing, gluing, and sewing. We girls help, too, though Mama does not want our schoolwork to suffer, so she will not let us stay up too late, and sends us up to bed.

The stress takes its toll. First Papa gets a cold, and as soon as he is better, Mama gets it, too. Kathleen and Michael come down with it at the same time. They have to stay home. I miss Michael's whistling and Kathleen's lilting speech. Sophie, Trudie, and I are lucky enough not to catch it, but poor Tania gets it worse than anyone else and runs a fever of one hundred and two. She has to miss school and stay in bed. I know Mama is worried about her. I can tell by the tight line of her mouth and the deep shadows under her eyes. Trudie and I take turns bringing Tania hot tea with honey and bowls of Mama's chicken soup. But Tania will not eat or drink. She clings to Shannon and calls for her mother. Yet even when a new letter comes—one of the thin, gray envelopes we know so well by now—she seems too agitated to read it, or even to have it read to her.

One morning just before Christmas, while Tania is still sick in bed, Papa asks me for Shannon—he has a meeting with Mr. Greenfield in a little while and he wants to bring the doll along. I creep into the room. Tania is asleep, and so I quietly take the doll from her arms and give it to Papa. "I'll be back before she gets up," he says.

When I get home from school, I hurry into the shop to see Papa. He is at his desk, with his big order sheet spread out in front of him.

"What did Mr. Greenfield say about Shannon?" I ask.

"He seemed to like her. But he said he was so busy now he couldn't think about her," Papa says. "He'll have to get back to me."

Oh. Well, at least he didn't say no outright. But I don't feel too hopeful. If he had really liked her, he would have said so right away.

"There's another problem," Papa says. "One of the buckles on the satchel isn't there. It must have gotten lost."

I remember how much Tania liked those buckles. But then I also remember there was a bunch of belts—and a bunch of buckles, too! Quickly, I locate the box, find the belt, and show the buckles to Papa. I am able to replace the buckle before Tania wakes and notices it is gone.

In the morning, Tania's fever has broken. She drinks a cup of tea and eats a piece of bread and jam. Mama is relieved. The worst, she says, is over. And soon, Christmas is over, too. All the dolls are delivered—barely!—in time, and Tania is better. She looks a bit pale after her sickness, but Mama assures us she will be all right.

I am glad we are all well again. All except Plucky.

I wonder where he is now? But there is no way of knowing. *Plucky*, I think as I walk to the library or to the grocery store for my mother. *Plucky, we're thinking of you. Stay safe. Stay strong.* Some people might think I am being foolish, talking in my head to a cat, especially one who is not even here. But I talk to my doll, don't I? So why not talk to a cat? It may not help. But then again, it can't hurt either.

# 12

## WINTER WONDERLAND

The month of February brings snow, snow, and more snow. Everything is transformed by the wonderful whiteness that pours down from the sky. It's as if all the everyday objects we know so well—a shop sign, a mail-box, a fire hydrant—have suddenly been covered with a coat of frosting. Because of the snow, school is closed on Thursday, a glorious day that we spend outside with all the children on our block who have come out to play. We make snow angels. We build snowmen, snow women, and snow children. We fashion forts and igloos and pelt each other with snowballs until we are so cold and wet that we simply have to get warm. Waving good-bye, everyone drifts back home.

But my sisters and I have fun inside, too. Mama makes cups of hot chocolate, into which she drops fat, pillowlike marshmallows. We pop kernels of corn on the stove. Sprinkled with salt and drizzled with melted butter, the popcorn is delicious. We bring our dolls out, too, and give them hot chocolate from the tea set we bought one year at F.A.O. Schwarz.

Even Sophie, who hasn't wanted to play dolls much lately, is willing today, especially when Mama gives us a bag of scraps from the furrier, Mr. Rosensweig, who has a shop on Orchard Street. Mama is friendly with his wife.

Sophie, Trudie, and I sew muffs for our dolls. Sophie's is dark brown, Trudie's is black, but mine is the best of all—pure white, like the snow. Of course the dolls have to model the muffs, and then we pretend they are all very fine ladies, strolling on Fifth Avenue in their real muffs, and their (imaginary) fur cloaks, and when they are tired, they take a carriage ride around Central Park.

It's only when we are finished with our game that I realize I have not seen Tania for hours, not since this morning. She played with us in the snow, though she went in earlier than we did. I thought that she was cold, and when she warmed up, she would come back outside. But she didn't.

"Have you seen her?" I ask Sophie.

"No, not for a while," Sophie says. We both look at Trudie, but she too shakes her head.

"Do you think we should go looking for her?" I ask.

But before anyone can answer, Papa comes in, stomping the snow off his boots and untying the long, woolly muffler Mama knit for him that is wrapped around his neck.

"Hello, hello, hello!" says Papa. Now he unbuttons his overcoat and shrugs it off. It seems like he is especially happy to be home.

"Hello, Papa," I say. "There was a snow day today. No school."

"That's news!" Papa says. "But I have even bigger news."

"Tell us," I say.

"I met with Mr. Greenfield today."

"Was it about Shannon?" I ask. Maybe Mr. Greenfield remembered her after all.

"Yes it was!" he exclaims. "Anna, Mr. Greenfield wants her for the store. He placed an order for fifty dolls. Fifty! Can you imagine?"

"He did?" I say. "I thought he wasn't very interested."

"That's what I thought, too. But then after the holiday, he found the buckle from the satchel! It was on the floor in his office. It reminded him about Shannon, and he started thinking about what a good idea it would be to have a schoolgirl doll. We're going to start making her right away. She'll be in the store by late summer, in time for the new school year."

"That's wonderful, Papa!" I say.

"I liked her right away," says Sophie. "I knew she was special." The admiring look in her eyes makes me feel very proud. And when Trudie breaks into her "happy dance," I am so happy that I join in.

"He thinks she is going to be a big success." Papa beams. "Now let's go upstairs and tell Mama." Papa bounds up the stairs and we follow.

Mama has made stew for dinner, and as she is ladling it into the blue-and-white bowls, we talk about the new doll and all the exciting plans Mr. Greenfield has for her.

It's only when everyone has been served that Mama comments on Tania's absence.

"Have any of you girls seen her?"

"No, Mama," I say. "We were just talking about that when Papa came home." Now I feel guilty. In my excitement about Shannon, I forgot all about Tania.

Mama gets up from the table and goes to the window. The snow, which had stopped for a few hours, has started falling again. "This is very strange," she says. "She usually is the first one at the table." And it's true. Now that Tania no longer hoards food, she eats with real appetite.

"Can we start?" Trudie asks. I am glad she asked. I'm worried about Tania, but all that time playing in the snow has made me very hungry.

Mama hesitates and then says, "Yes, girls. Go ahead and eat." We dig in, but Mama does not come back to the table right away. Instead, we hear her go into each of the other rooms, as well as the toilet in the hallway.

"Maybe she went out," says Mama when she returns to the kitchen alone.

She goes to the rack of hooks by the door. "Her coat isn't here," she says. "And Shannon wasn't on her bed."

Walking over to the window, Mama peers out as if she is searching for Tania in the swirling snow. "I'm going out to look for her."

"No, I'll go," says Papa. "You stay here with the girls."

"I hope she's all right," Trudie says.

"Me, too," adds Sophie.

"I'm sure she is," Papa says. He dips a heel of bread into the stew and then stands up and walks over to the coatrack.

"She's not a baby, after all," Mama says to no one in particular. It's as if she is trying to convince herself that Tania is all right. "She's a big girl."

*A big girl who doesn't speak much English*, I think but do not say. Why worry Mama any more than she is already worried? Suddenly, I have no more appetite. Even though the stew is delicious, I put down my fork and nudge the bowl away from me. Is it something we said or did that drove her away? I try to remember. Nothing jumps out at me. I had thought she was even feeling a little bit better about her life here. She seemed to love Ginger Cat so . . . Ginger Cat! Most nights, she comes up during dinner, winding herself around Tania's ankles in search of a tidbit. But tonight she's not here either. Could that be because she is where Tania is?

Suddenly, I jump up from the table. "Mama! I have an idea about where Tania might be," I say.

"You do? Then tell us right away."

"Come with me," I say. Everyone leaves their food and follows me downstairs. There is a big closet in the shop, where we used to keep some supplies. Since most of them are now kept on the shelves in the main room, only things we don't need too often are stored here, and the door is usually kept closed. It was closed today. I thought nothing of it. But now I think that the closet is a cozy, warm spot, perfect for reading, dreaming, playing games—or playing with a cat.

Sure enough, when we all troop downstairs and open the door, there is Tania, sitting on the footstool that was in her drawing. She looks startled to see us. Her coat is in a little heap on the floor. Shannon is sitting next to the coat, and Ginger Cat is curled up at her feet. She greets us with a soft mew. What a relief!

But even more astonishing is the fact that there in Tania's lap is Plucky. Plucky! He looks so sleek and well fed. And also calm. When I think of how desperate he seemed to get away when I caught him, I can't believe this is the same cat. But then he shifts a bit in Tania's lap, and I can see that his hind leg is missing. It is Plucky all right. But not the same Plucky we remember.

"Tania!" Mama exclaims. "We were so worried!" She drops to her knees in front of Tania, who begins speaking rapidly in Yiddish. Mama turns to us. "She was hiding because she didn't want Papa to know that she had brought Plucky inside. But she was worried about him out in the snow and didn't know what else to do."

Then Tania looks at Papa, and says very clearly: "Pluk-hee iz hap-hee!" She strokes his head and he yawns, a wide, sleepy cat-yawn.

A sentence. Tania has uttered an English sentence! I don't know if I am more astonished by that or by Plucky's transformation. His pale orange fur gleams, and he has lost the scrawny look that had me so worried.

"You did this?" I say to Tania. "You tamed him, fed him, groomed him all by yourself? How?"

"I luhk for Pluk-hee," Tania says slowly. "I find. I gif

him my luf. Many days. I feed, I pet, I speak mit soft voice. I know what it iz to luf a katz."

"Tania, that is wonderful. And wonderful that you can tell us about it in English. When did you learn to speak so well?" I knew she was saying some words but this—this is all new.

"I listen," Tania says. "All day. Hear words. Understand. But no say."

"You listened and understood, but you couldn't speak? Why, Tania?" I ask.

Tania doesn't answer, but looks down at the floor.

"You were too shy?" I say, beginning to understand. "You thought we would make fun of you?"

Still looking down, Tania nods.

"I guess Tania didn't need a teacher," Sophie says. "She taught herself."

"Yes!" I say. "She did." I turn to my father. "Papa, can you see the difference in Plucky?" Papa nods, clearly as amazed as the rest of us are. "It's Tania, Papa. Tania did this. She helped Plucky. He's a different cat now."

"It's true, it's true!" Trudie chimes in. "Please can we keep him, Papa? Please?"

And Sophie adds, "Plucky needs us, Papa. But Tania needs Plucky, too. Caring for the cat has helped her."

"He *is* like a different cat," Papa murmurs.

"And Tania is like a different child," adds Mama.

I can see what Mama means. Tania does look like a different girl from the one we first greeted. Her eyes— so very blue—are sparkling, and there is no trace of that awful blinking anymore. Even her posture seems different—straighter and taller. Best of all, she is smiling, really smiling, as she holds one cat and strokes the other.

Tania stands up and hands Plucky to Sophie. I feel a pang of worry. Will he claw or scratch? But he seems very content to be in Sophie's arms and nestles his creamy apricot head just under her chin.

"I think what Tania was able to do with Plucky was a fine thing," Papa says slowly. "But I don't like it that she disobeyed me. And I didn't want another cat. I made that very clear."

"So you won't let Plucky stay?" I say. Tears start welling up as I utter those words.

Papa looks at us. Can he see how much we all want Plucky to live here with us? Does he understand how important that is, not just to Tania, but to me as well? Before Papa can answer, Tania starts tugging on my hand. "Come," she says, so I follow her upstairs, through the apartment and into our room.

She leads me over to her bed and reaches for the pillow. My heart drops like a stone in a pond. The pillow—the pillow is ever so slightly lumpy. Is that because there is food underneath it? I thought all that was finished now.

But when Tania moves the pillow away, I don't see fruit or bread or eggs or rolls. I see a small, orange-colored toy cat. His face is made of fabric. His eyes are amber-colored buttons and his nose a tiny pink felt triangle. Black stitches form his whiskers, and a black ribbon is tied around his neck. It is the same ribbon I used to tie Shannon's braids. Tania must have found the scraps in the doll shop. The cat's body is made of soft, orangey fur. I remember there was a piece exactly that color in the bag of fur scraps.

"How did you do this?" I ask. "And when?"

"Today. After snow."

She did go in early, I remember. Way before the rest

of us. I look at the cat again and realize something else.

"Tania, this cat would be just the right size for Shan-non. He is Shannon's cat, isn't he?"

She nods. "Katz for Shannon."

"Well, Papa has got to see this!" I rush back down the stairs, clutching the cat in my hand. Tania is right behind me.

"Look!" I cry, bursting into the shop where my parents and sisters are still gathered. "Look at what Tania made!" I show the cat to Papa. "You see—a cat for Shannon.

And it's Plucky, Papa! It looks just like him!" Though I notice that Tania has cleverly gotten around the issue of the missing hind leg by only showing the cat's two front legs. The back ones have been gathered into a rounded shape underneath his tail.

"Let me see that," says Papa. He inspects the cat. "The scale is just right, isn't it?" he says, more to himself than to us. "A doll with her own satchel *and* her own pet cat. Now that's a good idea!"

"No, it's a marvelous, brilliant, perfect idea!" I say, and give Tania a big hug. For the first time, she hugs me right back.

"I think Greenfield will like it," Papa says. "In fact, I think he'll like it very much. I can't wait to show him."

"So does this mean Plucky can stay, Papa? Does it?" Trudie asks. She is hopping from one foot to another in her excitement. Not quite her happy dance. But almost.

"I can see he's been a good influence . . ." Papa begins. *Please, please, please let him say yes*, I pray. "But I don't like being disobeyed. Especially when Tania or one of you girls could have been hurt."

"We wanted to protect the girls," Mama says to Papa.

"But this time, they knew more than we did. Tania was right about Plucky. Just look."

"So you're willing to let him stay?" Papa says to Mama. "Even though we didn't want another cat?"

"Sometimes what you want can change," Mama says. "Especially when there are such good reasons." She looks at Tania and smiles.

"All right then," says Papa. His hand closes around the small orange cat Tania has made. "Plucky can stay."

He can stay! All of us—Sophie and Trudie, Tania, and I—break into the victory dance. Plucky can stay! Plucky can stay!

Papa reaches over to pat Plucky's head. Plucky's soft purring grows louder. "I guess Mama is right," Papa says. "Things *do* change. We didn't keep cats indoors in the old country. But this isn't the old country, is it girls? This is the new country. Our new home. And in our new home, cats get to live inside."

"We luf Pluk-hee," Tania says. She has stopped dancing and sounds almost solemn. I understand. Love is big. It can make you feel that way.

"And Ginger Cat, too," I add. I glance out the window

to the street, where the snow continues to fall in fat, white flakes. There will be even more snow on the ground by tomorrow. A whole world of snow to play in, romp in, jump in, dance in. And when, at the end of the day, we're shivering and wet, with raw cheeks and stone-cold toes, we'll come back inside, where it's safe and warm, and where the cats in the doll shop will be curled up and waiting—just for us.

# AUTHOR'S NOTE

Many years ago, my husband and I lived in an apartment on Second Avenue and Eighty-fourth Street in New York City. Our kitchen window faced a drab, dark yard of little interest to either of us. Although some of the neighboring apartments had terraces, no one actually used them. They became a kind of outdoor storage area for most of the tenants, and they were heaped with unwanted items: a lamp with no shade, an unused bicycle, a broken chair. But when a stray cat decided to have her kittens in the bottom drawer of an abandoned dresser, my husband and I suddenly grew very interested in the view out back.

We followed the doings of the new family of felines eagerly, but were horrified when the owner of the bureau—the true-life inspiration for the man with the mustache—swept the kittens from her terrace with a broom. One of the kittens, a little orange-colored male, broke his leg in the fall. We wanted to help him, but we had no access to the yard into which he had fallen. We set out food on our fire escape for his mother and siblings, who were able to come over and eat it. But the wounded kitten could not climb over the fence that separated our yards, nor could he clamber up the fire escape stairs like his mother and sister. We worried about what would become of him.

We watched, first with sorrow, but soon with growing awe and pride, how the broken limb eventually dropped off and the kitten learned to navigate his world on his remaining three legs. He scrambled around in search of the food we tossed over the fence, and he grew into a spunky fellow who brought a special joy to our days.

The memory of that resilient little cat stayed with me for years, and I wrote about him in a brief children's tale that I shared with my superlative Viking editor, Joy Peskin. When Joy read it, she immediately thought of the doll shop family and suggested that I incorporate his hope-filled story into that of the Breittlemanns and their Russian cousin. It is my wish that the resulting book—*The Cats in the Doll Shop*—will give readers a strong sense of both the brave little cat that inspired it and the equally brave fictional girls who helped him along on his journey.

# GLOSSARY OF TERMS

BUBBE—Yiddish term for Grandma.

CHALLAH—Traditional Jewish egg bread made in a braided loaf on Shabbas and in a round loaf on Rosh Hashanah.

CHANUKAH—The Jewish festival of lights, lasting eight days and eight nights.

DREIDEL—A four-sided wooden top with a Hebrew letter on each side. Dreidels are used in a game of chance during the festival of Chanukah.

EREV—Evening, in Yiddish; used to refer to the day before a holiday, or the evening of Shabbas.

GEFILTE FISH—Fish balls or patties made of carp or pike that are traditionally eaten on Shabbas or other holidays.

GELT—A Yiddish term for money.

KUGEL—A Jewish pudding made with potatoes or egg noodles.

LATKE—A fried patty of potato and onion, traditionally served at Chanukah.

MENORAH—The nine-branched candelabrum used on Chanukah.

ROSH HASHANAH—The Jewish New Year; it usually comes in September.

SHABBAS—The weekly Jewish day of rest, which begins at sundown on Friday. No work is done on that day.

TOCHTER—Yiddish for "daughter"; also used as a term of endearment.

TZEDAKAH—The Jewish concept of charity; giving to the needy and the poor.

TZIMMES—A traditional Jewish dish made with carrots and raisins or prunes, often served on Rosh Hashanah.

YOM KIPPUR—The day of atonement in the Jewish calendar, which occurs ten days after Rosh Hashanah. Traditionally, adults fast for the entire day, but children are not required to.

# TIMELINE

1820–1930—It is estimated that as many as 4.5 million Irish immigrants arrived in America during this period. Kathleen and Michael O'Leary came over as part of this mass emigration.

1870—Opening of F.A.O. Schwarz, the world famous toy store, at Broadway and Ninth Street in New York City. The store made several moves over the years, and had different homes including Fifth Avenue and Thirty-first Street, and Fifth Avenue and Fifty-eighth Street. The present store is located at Fifth Avenue and Fifty-ninth Street.

1885—The popcorn cart is invented. The new steam and gas poppers were easy to push through parks, fairs, carnivals and expositions, and as a result, popcorn became a popular snack.

1886—The Statue of Liberty is dedicated. The people of France gave the statue to the people of the United States in recognition of the friendship between the two countries, a friendship that began during the American Revolution. Over the years, the statue has come to stand for freedom and democracy for all people.

1892—Opening of Ellis Island in New York. For millions of immigrants, this was the first stop in America. Like Anna's parents, many of these immigrants were from Russia. Other immigrants came from Poland, Italy, Germany, Norway, Ireland, and all over the world.

1904—The Tompkins Square branch of the New York Public Library opens at 331 East Tenth Street in New York City. The library still stands in the exact same location today.

1914—World War I breaks out in Europe.

1917—United States enters World War I; Russian Revolution breaks out.

1918—World War I ends; peace treaty signed by the Allies and Germany.

*Turn the page*
for a sample of the first story
about Anna and her family . . .

*The*
# DOLL SHOP
*Downstairs*

# I

## ℳEET THE DOLLS

"Don't push!" I tell my little sister, Trudie.

"I'm not pushing, Anna," says Trudie. "You are!"

"If you two fight, Mama will make us go back upstairs," says our big sister, Sophie. Sophie is eleven, but right now she is talking to us like she is a grown-up and we are just babies. Well, maybe she thinks Trudie is a baby, but *I'm* not, so I wish she would stop using that tone.

Sophie, Trudie, and I have spent most of the afternoon cleaning the doll repair shop our parents own and run. Now we are allowed to stay in the shop to play. But Sophie is right: if we quarrel, Mama will hear us and make us come upstairs. So I let Trudie go ahead, even if she does shove her way in front of me and step on my foot besides. Trudie *is* only seven so I suppose I should be understanding.

I've always lived above the doll shop on Essex Street. Mama says that a long time ago, when Sophie was a baby, the three of them lived in a different apartment, on Ludlow Street. But to me, Ludlow Street doesn't count. It's Essex Street, and only Essex Street, that is home. Out in front there is a sign that reads:

**BREITTLEMANN'S DOLL REPAIR**
All Kinds of Dolls Lovingly Restored and Mended
*Established 1904*

Underneath the letters is a picture of a smiling doll. Mama painted it. She can paint a picture of anything. She is the one who paints the dolls' faces—the rosy cheeks, the red lips—so well that you'd never know they weren't brand new. I tell her I think she is a magician, but she only smiles and keeps her hand steady on the brush.

Trudie runs ahead of me and reaches for "her" doll, which is made of bisque and has thick, dark hair. The doll is not really hers, of course. All the dolls here are waiting to be fixed by Papa. But while they wait, he

lets us play with them. We each choose a single doll at a time—that's the rule—and we have to be careful when we play. The dolls are very fragile and easy to break. The only time a doll can leave the shop is with its owner. We are not owners. We have no bisque or china dolls that belong to just us. Bisque and china dolls are expensive. We used to have rag dolls that Mama made, but they have fallen apart from so much use, and she has not had a chance to make new ones. Papa says that if the shop does really, really well, one day he will buy each of us a doll of our own. But it seems to me that day is a long way off.

"Angelica Grace!" breathes Trudie when she sees her doll. Angelica Grace is a name Sophie came up with. She read it in a book and told it to Trudie. Sophie comes up with all the names for our dolls—she's good at that, but then, she is good at so many things.

Compared to some of the other dolls in the shop, Angelica Grace doesn't look too bad. Her navy pleated skirt and white sailor blouse are only a little wrinkled. Her hair is neat. She even has navy leather shoes and white ribbed stockings on her feet. But one of her blue glass eyes is missing, and there is a big, dark hole where it once was. It makes her look kind of spooky.

Sophie's current doll—she calls her Victoria Marie—looks much worse. The toes of her bare feet are broken, and her blonde hair is always tangled, though Sophie tries to comb it. All of her clothes are missing. But she has the sweetest smile, and tiny holes in her earlobes where real earrings can fit.

The doll that is "mine" is Bernadette Louise. Her face, legs, and arms are made of shiny glazed porcelain. Her dark hair is painted on and decorated with beautiful painted blue flowers. Mama says they are morning glories. On one foot, she wears a black painted boot with a blue tassled garter; the other foot is missing. Her dark red and gold flowered skirt must have been nice once, but it is now torn and stained. Her right arm is badly cracked.

One day, I asked Papa why these three dolls were still in the shop. Usually he mends the dolls promptly and then sends them home again.

"Which dolls?" he asked, and I showed him the three dolls we thought of as "ours."

"I'm having trouble getting the right color eye for this doll," Papa said, pointing to Angelica Grace. "The blues I find are always wrong." He frowned slightly. "But I keep trying. One day, I'll find an eye that's a perfect match."

"And the others?"

"Well, the owners of this doll," he said, looking at Victoria Marie, "told me they were going on a long trip. No one will be able to pick the doll up for quite a while so there's no rush in fixing her." He smoothed the doll's tangled hair gently. "Now this doll," he said, picking up Bernadette Louise and looking into her face, "is very old—much older than the other two. Getting the right parts for her has been very difficult. They don't make legs or arms the way they used to; I keep hoping I'll find the perfect ones. But so far, I haven't."

Sometimes, Papa can fix a broken part with his file or one of his other tools. But when he can't fix a part, he has to get a new one. He orders them all the way from Germany, where most of the dolls are made. The doll parts arrive in huge boxes brought by the postman, Mr. Greevy.

Sophie, Trudie, and I are always thrilled when a box arrives, and if we are not in school, we stop whatever we are doing to help Papa open and sort through it. Inside, there are doll arms and legs of different sizes and shapes, all packed in straw and shredded paper. There are lots of wigs—blonde, brown, red, black; braids, buns, curls. Doll bodies are in the box, too, and sometimes clothes. Even though Mama could make or repair anything, a customer sometimes requests a special outfit. Once we found a doll-sized fancy gray silk ball gown and matching evening coat. Another time, there was a satin bridal dress with a train, veil, and the most adorable tiny white leather gloves.

But the very best things in the box are the glass eyes. Because they are so fragile, the eyes are packed first in tissue, then straw, and then finally in their own tiny boxes. Each glass eye is a hollow white ball with a different color in the center. Some are dark, inky blue, while others are sky blue, chocolate brown, amber, or green.

"I wish our dolls had a bed," says Trudie now, the whine just beginning to creep into her voice. Sophie, who has found Victoria Marie and is busy trying to smooth out her hair, ignores her. "We need a bed." Now Trudie really is whining.

I want to shake her. But if I do, I will get in trouble with Mama. So instead, I say, "Guess what? We *have* a bed."

"We do?" Trudie asks, eyes wide. Even Sophie looks interested. "Where is it?"

"Right here!" I say, and drag something out from behind the glass-topped counter.

"Oh!" breathes Trudie when she sees it. Of course, if you didn't know, the thing I dragged out might not look much like a bed at all, and instead might seem to be an ordinary wooden box. In fact, it is a box, given to me by Mr. Bloom, who owns the grocery shop on the corner. The box originally held vegetables but now that it was empty, Mr. Bloom was happy to give it to me. Made of smooth golden wood, the box is deep and sturdy. As soon as I saw it, I knew it was a perfect place for three dolls to spend the night.

"That was a good idea, Anna," Sophie says. I stand up a little straighter when she says that. Even though Sophie can annoy me by being so very perfect, her praise still matters. She doesn't give me much of it, either.

"Go ahead, put her in," urges Sophie, and Trudie places her doll in the bottom of the box. Sophie and I do the same. Then Trudie bursts out, "But we don't have a blanket! How can they sleep without a blanket?"

"You don't have to cry," says Sophie. "I have a blanket."

"Where? Where is it? I want to see!" says Trudie. I'm curious, too. What does Sophie have in mind?

"Here," Sophie says, and she pulls something white and soft from the pocket of her apron.

"A pillow case!" says Trudie. "How perfect!" She gazes up adoringly at Sophie. "You always know how to fix things," she adds. Somehow, this makes me feel cross. Trudie didn't get all *that* excited over the bed that I found for us; it's always Sophie this, Sophie that, Sophie, Sophie, Sophie.

"Where did you get it?" I ask.

"From Mama's rag basket," says Sophie.

Then she tucks the pillowcase up around the dolls' chins.

"Will she mind?"

"No, silly! It's a rag." Sophie uses that superior, I'm-so-grown-up voice again.

"Can we leave them in the box all night?" asks Trudie, sounding worried.

"Yes," says Sophie. "They'll be safe. I promise."

"Good night, Angelica Grace," says Trudie. She leans over to kiss her doll, loudly, on the cheek.

"Good night," says Sophie to her own doll as she and Trudie head for the stairs. "Are you coming?" she asks me. Even though she has put the light out, I can feel her looking at me.

"In a minute," I tell her.

She doesn't say anything else but just takes Trudie's hand and goes upstairs.

I listen to their footsteps as they go, but I don't follow them right away. I want to be alone down here for a little bit. Sometimes it's hard being a middle sister, and I just need to be by myself.